"You've changed."

That was all he'd said. And, he might have added, not for the better.

Jenny had to blink rapidly to banish the stinging in her eyes. She was *not* going to cry.

Had she really changed so much? She jerked down the windshield visor, staring at her reflection in the lighted mirror there. The answer to her question stared back at her. It was hard to find even a trace of the girl she'd been ten years before. Jenny wondered if she even existed anymore.

"Idiot." She snapped the visor back into place and reached for the ignition key. What was she thinking of? Why should she care what Mitch Sullivan thought of how she looked? Of course he was disappointed, She was no longer the silly little girl who'd hung on his every word. And it didn't look as if he'd changed much. He was probably the same hell-raiser he'd always been.

The same man who'd left Ransome, Colorado, ten years before.

The same man who'd left *her* ten years before.

Dear Reader,

Once again Intimate Moments is offering you a month filled with terrific books, starting right off with Kathleen Korbel's American Hero title, *A Walk on the Wild Side*. J. P. O'Neill is an undercover agent for the DEA, but when he's framed for the murder of his partner, he realizes his own agency has set him up. The only thing to do is take off in search of the truth himself, and the only way to escape is in the company of his lawyer—who's handcuffed to his arm! Theirs is a rocky beginning, but the end will be terrific—if only they can live that long!

In *The Hell-Raiser,* author Dallas Schulze pens a powerful tale of lovers reunited after ten long years. Jenny had always been the proverbial good girl and Mitch the bad boy, but now he feels it's time for her to let go of the guilts of the past and let him take her for a whirl through life.

Linda Shaw's *Indian Summer* takes a hero and heroine from feuding families and forces them into an alliance that is at first just business but eventually becomes something far more: love. As always, Linda plumbs the depths of her characters' hearts—and souls.

In *Run to the Moon,* talented Sandy Steen puts her own unique spin on the ever-popular "secret baby" plot, while Catherine Palmer's *Red Hot* takes you to chile farm country for a steamy marriage-of-convenience story. Finally, let new author Julia Quinn tell you about *Wade Conner's Revenge*. Driven from town by suspicion and unprovable accusations, betrayed by the silence of the woman he loved, Wade Conner returns with a score to settle. But suspicion begins to follow him once again, and now he needs the help of a woman he no longer trusts—to keep a murder charge at bay.

I think you'll enjoy each and every one of these terrific books, as well as all the exciting novels we have in store for you in months to come—books by such favorites as Rachel Lee, Marilyn Pappano, Paula Detmer Riggs and Justine Davis, to name only a few. Meanwhile, happy reading!

Yours,

Leslie J. Wainger
Senior Editor and Editorial Coordinator

THE HELL-RAISER

Dallas Schulze

Published by Silhouette Books New York
America's Publisher of Contemporary Romance

SILHOUETTE BOOKS
300 East 42nd St., New York, N.Y. 10017

THE HELL-RAISER

ISBN: 0-373-07462-X

First Silhouette Books printing November 1992

Printed in the U.S.A.

DALLAS SCHULZE

loves books, old movies, her husband and her cat, not necessarily in that order. She's a sucker for a happy ending, whose writing has given her an outlet for her imagination and hopes that readers have half as much fun with her books as she does! Dallas has more hobbies than there is space to list them, but is currently working on a doll collection.

Chapter 1

"Come on, baby. You know you want to." There was a definite threat beneath the coaxing tone.

"All I want to do is go home, Brad." Jenny Monroe blocked his attempt to put his hand on her breast and told herself that there was nothing to be afraid of. She'd known Brad most of her life. They'd been in the same class since second grade. It wasn't as if he would hurt her or...something.

"I'll take you home after you give me a little reward. Come on, Jen, what's the big deal? It isn't like I haven't kissed you before."

"If I let you kiss me, will you take me home?" She eyed him suspiciously in the light from the dashboard.

"Sure, baby."

She didn't want to kiss him. She would have preferred whacking him over the head for drinking too much at the party and behaving like a jerk now. But she was ten miles from home and it was almost ten o'clock. She was tired, and this wrestling match with Brad was an unpleasant way to end the evening.

"One kiss," she said, not bothering to conceal her annoyance. "And then you take me home and you go somewhere and sober up."

Brad didn't bother answering. He dragged her close, oblivious to the fact that the gearshift dug painfully into her leg, and plastered his mouth over hers. Jenny tried to relax, reminding herself that she'd enjoyed Brad's kisses in the past. But she'd never been coerced into accepting them before.

When he tried to shove his tongue into her mouth, she clamped her teeth together and turned her head aside.

"That's enough, Brad."

"No, it's not. Not near enough." His voice was slurred, his breath sour from the beer he'd drunk earlier.

"Yes, it is." Jenny's hands pushed against his shoulders as he tried to kiss her again. It was like pushing against a granite boulder. How often had she admired Brad's heavily muscled shoulders and chest? Jenny didn't feel any admiration now.

"Let me go."

"Come on, baby. Don't be such a little prude." Denied access to her mouth, Brad contented himself with leaving a trail of wet kisses down the side of her neck.

"Let me go!" The beginnings of fear made her voice sharp.

When Brad's only response was to close his hand over her breast and squeeze painfully hard, Jenny lost her battle to stay calm. She was no longer at all sure that he wouldn't hurt her. She was already going to have bruises from his rough handling, and he didn't seem to have any intention of stopping.

Twisting her head to the side, she fastened her teeth on his wrist and bit down. Hard.

"Ow!" Brad howled with pain and jerked away. "You little bitch!" Jenny didn't wait to hear anything more. She wrenched the passenger door open and all but fell out onto the graveled road.

She was wearing a skinny little dress that had seemed just right for the party. It was not, however, warm enough for a June night in the foothills of Colorado's Rockies. She shivered as the cool air hit her bare arms.

But catching a chill was the least of her worries, she realized. She'd thought that, given a few seconds to cool off, Brad would realize how wrong he'd been. But he didn't look in the least apologetic as he loomed up on his side of the sports car.

A full moon hung low in the clear sky, casting deep shadows over the road but providing enough light for Jenny to see the anger that turned Brad's even features into a frightening mask.

He started around the hood and Jenny backed away, her heart pounding. She'd never been quite so aware of the sheer physical disadvantages a woman faced in any physical contest that pitted her against a man. If Brad caught her, she'd be helpless.

"Brad, calm down." Her voice shook. "You've been drinking."

"Worried that I can't perform?" He grinned, his teeth gleaming in the moonlight. "Don't worry, you won't be disappointed, baby."

"Brad, I don't want to sleep with you." Jenny backed around the rear of the car.

"Who said anything about sleeping?" He leered at her, obviously thinking he'd said something clever.

Jenny cast a frantic look around, but there was nothing to be seen but empty countryside. Why hadn't she protested when Brad took the cutoff? *Because it hadn't occurred to her that he was capable of acting like this.*

Her fingers trailing along the side of the car, Jenny continued to back away. Her mind worked frantically, trying to find some way to stop this cat-and-mouse game. It was Brad who ended it but not in the way Jenny had wanted.

She cried out, startled, as he suddenly lunged toward her, his arms outstretched. She tried to dart away, but the gravel made a poor running surface and her high heels made lousy track shoes. Her feet slipped, and only by grabbing the fender of the car did she avoid falling. Before she had a chance to try again, Brad was on her.

His big hands were hard and hurting as he caught her by the arm and spun her around to face him. He jerked her against his chest, the impact momentarily knocking the wind out of her.

"No! Let me go!" She fought to get her hands between them, but she was unable to push him away.

"I'll let you go when I'm through with you." He wrapped one arm across her back, crushing her against him. His other hand found her thigh, sliding up under the brief skirt.

Sobbing with fear, Jenny tried to bring her knee up, but he twisted so that the blow landed on his thigh. The impact made Brad grunt with pain but he didn't loosen his hold.

"You're such a snotty little bitch." His hand closed over her buttock, squeezing painfully hard as he dragged her up against him. "Think you're better than everyone else just because your daddy is Willard Monroe."

"No, I don't. I don't think I'm better than you." Jenny twisted frantically, trying to break his hold. But her struggles only seemed to force her closer to him.

"Think you're too good to put out, don't you?" Brad wrapped his hand in her hair and jerked her head back.

Jenny stared up at him, seeing nothing of the boy she'd thought she knew. It wasn't the moonlight that cast his face into a twisted mask. It was drink and lust and an anger she didn't understand.

"Brad, please. Don't do this." She didn't care that she was begging. She just wanted him to let her go. She wanted this terrifying scene to end. But she might as well have been pleading with one of the cottonwood trees that lined the road.

"You're going to like it, baby," Brad told her. He rocked his hips against her, his arousal hard and frightening even through the layers of clothing.

"I'm not going to like it. And I hate being called 'baby'!" she added irrelevantly.

She jerked wildly against him. The abrupt movement took him off guard, serving to loosen his hold slightly. It was enough to give her room to draw her foot back and land a kick against his shin. The blow probably hurt her toes more than his leg but his hands slackened for a moment, giving her a chance to slip away.

She stumbled back, her breath coming deep and hard. There was nowhere to hide, nowhere to run. As Brad started toward her, she knew that the end of this little chase was inevitable. She couldn't outrun him. She was certainly no match for him in any kind of physical struggle. And words didn't seem to be reaching him.

"I don't mind if you want to play games, baby." Brad grinned at her. "We can play chase if you want."

She didn't waste her breath answering him. Maybe if she could stay out of his reach long enough, he'd come to his senses. It was a thin hope on both counts. It wasn't likely that she could outmaneuver the best tackle Ransome High had seen in years. Nor did she really believe that Brad was going to suddenly change back into the boy she'd thought she knew.

Before she was forced to find out, she heard a vehicle approaching. She turned her head toward the sound, hope welling up in her chest. If she could get the driver to stop, she could bring an end to this nightmare.

But Brad had heard it, too. Taking advantage of her distraction, he lunged forward and caught her by the arm. Jenny cried out as he began to pull her toward the car. If he dragged her behind it, there would be no reason for the other driver to stop. And then, nothing would prevent Brad from raping her.

Rape. For the first time, she consciously faced what he was going to do to her. It seemed incredible that someone she'd known all her life could do something so terrible. But this wasn't the boy she'd known. This was someone capable of violence, capable of hurting her. Someone capable of rape.

The sound of the approaching engine was loud in her ears. In another moment, Brad would have forced her behind the car, out of sight of the road, unable to summon help. She had to break free. And she had to do it now.

She'd been dragging back against his hold, fighting every inch of forward movement. Now she lunged toward him, bringing up her free hand and raking her nails across his face. The sudden shift in tactics threw him momentarily off balance, loosening his grip enough for her to jerk free.

Sobbing, Jenny stumbled away from him and dashed around the car. She slid to a halt in the middle of the gravel road, throwing one arm up to shield her eyes as light slashed across her face.

A motorcycle. And it was much closer than she'd realized. So close that it seemed as if only a miracle could prevent it from crashing into her. For a split second, she stood in the roadway, pinned in the light, as incapable of movement as if she were a doe caught in the headlights of a car. She couldn't even close her eyes, but instead she stared at the big bike in fascinated horror, waiting for the impact.

And then the bike was wrenched to the side with brutal strength. It skidded past, so close it nearly brushed against her. Gravel spun beneath the wheels, pelting Jenny's bare legs with stinging blows as she spun to watch the inevitable crash. The bike slid across the road, almost horizontal as it headed for the ditch. But at the last possible second, just when it seemed that it would skid off the road, the rider dragged it up, the rear wheel fishtailing violently as he brought the bike to a sliding halt, still upright.

The engine's roar cut off so suddenly that Jenny felt almost dizzy in the abrupt silence that followed. For the space of several seconds, she could only think of how grateful she was that she hadn't caused an accident. But then she heard Brad move behind her and she was reminded of the reason she'd run into the road in the first place.

She moved toward the motorcycle.

"Come back here!" Brad's barked order only made Jenny move faster.

The motorcycle's rider booted the kickstand into place and swung off the bike, turning toward her. Jenny stopped so quickly that one foot slid on the loose gravel.

Mitchell Sullivan. She should have realized who he was from the bike. She'd seen it roaring through town often enough. He worked at Eddie's Garage as a mechanic, but some people thought his main occupation was raising hell. If there was trouble in Ransome, Mitch was likely to be smack in the middle of it.

He'd been arrested a few times but never for anything more serious than a drunk-and-disorderly charge. He'd been in more brawls than you could shake a stick at, and according to rumor, when he wasn't getting in a fight, he was probably parked somewhere with some girl who ought to know better.

Jenny had never met Mitch, but she knew all about his reputation. In a town the size of Ransome, a man like Mitch Sullivan provided plenty of grist for the gossip mill.

"Is there a problem, or do you just have a thing about trying to kill motorcycle riders?" It was the first time she'd heard his voice. The deep, raspy tones sounded as dangerous as he looked.

"I'm sorry." She hovered in the roadway, caught between the frying pan and the fire.

The full moon painted everything in shades of gray, but it cast enough light to give Mitch a clear view of the girl in the middle of the road.

He'd seen her around town, though they'd never met. Of course, everyone knew who she was. Willard Monroe's daughter was as much a personage in her way as Mitch himself was. Since Monroe Furniture Works provided most of the jobs in town, either directly or indirectly, the Monroe family was well-known.

Jenny, he thought her name was. Probably a high school senior by now. Honey-blond hair, big brown eyes and legs that went on forever. The sort of girl a man just couldn't help but notice even when she was far beyond his reach.

But she didn't look much like the confident girl he'd seen around town. She stood in the middle of the empty road, her eyes wide. She was wearing a flouncy little black dress. The soft fabric was crushed, one sleeve torn at the shoulder. Mitch didn't think it was the moonlight that made her cheeks look pale and her eyes frightened.

And he didn't have far to look for the cause of that pallor and the fear in her eyes. Brad Louderman was striding toward her, his square-featured face ugly in the oddly clear light.

"Get on. I'll take you home."

Jenny stared at the gloved hand he held out, hesitating a moment longer. All she knew about Mitch Sullivan was his reputation, which wasn't good. But she'd never heard rumors that he'd ravished any of the seemingly endless stream of women he'd dated.

She took a step forward only to find she'd hesitated too long. Brad's fingers closed over her arm, making it clear that the delay hadn't cooled his temper any. Any lingering doubts she might have had about the wisdom of accepting Mitch's offer of a ride vanished. At least there was no reason to think that he meant her any harm. With Brad, there was no question.

She pulled against Brad's hold, only to gasp when he tightened his grip, deliberately hurting her.

"Get lost, Sullivan," he snapped. "Nobody's taking Jenny anywhere."

"I think she should decide that for herself." Mitch closed the distance between them in three long strides. "Let her go."

"This isn't any of your business, Sullivan." Brad's voice held a challenge. The two of them were well matched in size, but Mitch was older and Brad knew his reputation for being a wicked fighter as well as Jenny did. However, Brad was in a belligerent mood, and he'd had enough to drink to make him feel a little reckless.

"Let her go." Mitch didn't raise his voice. He sounded as calm as if the three of them were having a chat after church. He reached out and caught Brad's wrist in his hand. Jenny didn't see him exert any pressure, but the color suddenly drained from Brad's face.

"Let her go," Mitch said again, his tone almost gentle. "Now."

With a low obscenity, Brad's fingers dropped away from Jenny's arm. Since she'd been hanging back against his hold, Jenny stumbled slightly when he released her. The arm that caught her around the waist was hard as a rock. Mitch steadied her easily, his eyes never leaving Brad's face. Jenny realized that he hadn't released his grasp on the younger man's wrist.

"Did he hurt you?"

It took her a moment to realize that the question was directed at her. She touched her tongue to the inside of her lower lip and tasted blood where Brad's mouth had crushed the delicate skin. But that wasn't what Mitch meant.

"No, not really." Jenny was startled by the shakiness of her own voice. She cleared her throat and tried to sound a little more sure. "I'm okay."

"Shall I beat him to a pulp for you?" Mitch asked conversationally.

Jenny saw Brad's eyes bulge and his mouth open as if to protest, but no sound came out. Whatever the hold was that Mitch had on his arm, it seemed to be powerful enough to discourage him from trying to break away. Remembering how badly he'd frightened her, Jenny let the moment stretch, thinking almost wistfully of how nice it would be to see Brad's face pounded to a pulp.

"No," she said when she'd let him suffer a little. "He's not worth it."

"You're lucky, Louderman. I'd like nothing more than to see you grovel. But since the lady doesn't feel the same, I'll let you off with a warning. If I ever see you near her again, I won't be nearly so nice."

"You can't tell me what to do," Brad said, but his loud tone couldn't conceal the uneasiness in his eyes.

"I *am* telling you." Mitch's voice was almost a whisper, the softness somehow more threatening than if he'd shouted.

"And the next time you feel like experimenting with attempted rape, you might want to give some thought to how few eunuchs there are playing professional football these days."

His voice remained pleasant, but glancing at his face, Jenny had to suppress a shiver. She'd never in her life seen such cold danger in a man's eyes. But she'd also never felt anything more reassuring than the steady arm he kept around her waist.

Brad must have seen the same threat. The aggression drained from his face, leaving him looking suddenly a good deal smaller. He was outmatched and they all knew it.

"You can't threaten me," he said weakly.

"I just have," Mitch pointed out politely. Without another word, he turned his back on Brad and led Jenny to where the motorcycle sat.

If he gave any thought to the possibility that Brad might attack him from behind, Jenny saw no indication of it. She did her best to appear as unconcerned as her rescuer. If you didn't count her shaking knees, perhaps she succeeded.

She heard the sound of Brad's car door as they reached the bike. The engine had barely caught when he slammed it into gear. Gravel spun beneath the tires, seeking purchase on the ground beneath. An instant later, the car roared by. Neither she nor Mitch spoke until the taillights had disappeared around a shallow curve.

"I don't think you have to worry about him bothering you again."

"Thank you." She felt a pang of regret when his arm slid from her waist. Forcing strength into knees that felt like warm Jell-O, she turned to look at him. "I really appreciate you coming to my rescue."

"No problem." He shrugged, his mouth twisting in a grin. "I live to do good deeds."

Jenny smiled uncertainly, remembering some of the stories she'd heard about him. Good deeds rarely figured in those stories.

"Come on, let's get you home."

Jenny had never been on a motorcycle in her life. She'd always thought they looked rather wicked and exciting. But, somehow, climbing onto Mitch Sullivan's bike felt more safe and secure than exciting. Or maybe it was Mitch who made it feel that way.

"Put your arms around my waist and just hold on," he told her over his shoulder. Tentatively Jenny did as he told her, setting her hands gingerly against his sides, sitting carefully upright behind him.

But she forgot all about keeping her distance when he turned into the first curve. Feeling the bike tilt and seeing the ground seemingly only inches from her leg, Jenny was suddenly more concerned with survival than propriety.

Mitch grinned to himself as he felt her slim arms abruptly circle his waist, her hands clasping above his belt buckle. She pressed herself against his back, her face buried in the leather of his jacket.

She had guts, he thought, his smile fading. She hadn't collapsed into tears once the danger had lifted. Not that he'd have blamed her if she had. Near rape was worth a few tears.

He was rather sorry he'd let Brad Louderman off as easily as he had. He knew Louderman's type. He had little patience with spoiled young men who thought they had the right to take what they wanted, no matter who they hurt.

It was a good thing he'd come along when he had. He didn't like to think of what would have happened to Jenny Monroe if he hadn't. She seemed like a nice enough kid. She didn't put on the kind of airs you might expect from Willard Monroe's only child.

If she hadn't been so far beyond his reach, he might have thought about looking her up in a couple of weeks, asking her out, maybe seeing what those brown eyes looked like when they were smiling. Mitch shrugged the thought off. Even if she hadn't been a Monroe, she was too young for him. He was nearly twenty-six, too old to be dating seventeen-year-old girls, even ones as pretty as this one.

Jenny didn't lift her head from its safe hiding place on Mitch's shoulder until she felt the bike slow. Raising her head, she saw that they'd reached the end of the long circular driveway that led up to her home.

"Just drop me off here," she told him, raising her voice to be heard over the sound of the engine. She felt him hesitate a moment, but to her relief, he stopped the bike and shut it off.

Nudging the kickstand into place, he slid from the bike and then turned to offer her a hand in getting off. Standing in front of him, Jenny hesitated, looking for the right words to express her gratitude.

"I wouldn't worry about it," he said abruptly. "I doubt anyone saw us together."

He'd settled back onto the bike and was reaching for the key before Jenny realized what he was talking about. He thought she didn't want him to take her to the door because she didn't want her parents to see her with him.

"Wait." She reached out and caught hold of his arm. "I don't care if anyone sees us together." She'd recovered enough from her experience with Brad to sound indignant.

"Don't you?" Mitch slanted her a skeptical look.

"No. I just don't want to have to explain things to my parents. If they hear your bike, they might ask questions. You know, like why didn't Brad bring me home."

To her relief, he lowered his hand from the key and relaxed back on the seat. "Aren't you going to tell them what happened with Mr. Captain-of-the-Football-Team?"

She looked at the ground and shook her head. "I don't think so."

"Why not? Don't you think they'd want to know?"

No, she didn't. At least her mother wouldn't. The Loudermans were one of the few families in Ransome that Stephanie Monroe considered nearly her social equals. She'd been pleased when Jenny and Brad started dating. She would not be pleased when she found out that they'd broken up. And if Jenny told her why, she'd probably think it was something Jenny had done that caused Brad to act the way he had. But she couldn't tell Mitch Sullivan that.

"He didn't really hurt me." She shrugged to show that the incident was hardly worth thinking about.

"Didn't he?" Mitch cupped her chin in his hand and lifted her face to his. His thumb brushed over her swollen lip. The gentle touch made Jenny's eyes sting with tears. She blinked them back and forced a shaky smile.

"Well, he didn't hurt me much," she amended. "I just don't want to go through all the explanations and junk."

"Your choice." She could feel his eyes studying her face and hoped the moonlight didn't reveal how shaken she still felt. "I don't think you'll have any trouble with Louderman, but if you do, let me know."

"Thank you." This time her smile was a bit steadier. "I don't think you're nearly as bad as people say."

"Thanks. I think." Mitch's mouth curved in a rueful smile.

"You're welcome." Though there was no reason to stay, Jenny lingered, somehow reluctant to end the moment.

Mitch's hand lifted again, his fingers brushed her tender mouth. The soft touch seemed to take away the sting of her split lip. Jenny stared, mesmerized, as he leaned forward, his hand slipping around to cup the back of her neck. Her eyes fluttered shut just as his mouth touched hers.

It was a light kiss, soft as a rose petal, meant only to offer comfort, ending almost as soon as it began. Jenny sighed, feeling an odd disappointment. Light has the kiss had been, it seemed to hold a promise of so much more. Her lashes lifted as Mitch drew back. She stared into his eyes, wishing that the moonlight was brighter.

"Just to remind you that it isn't always nasty," Mitch said with a half smile.

"Thank you." She couldn't think of anything else to say.

"My pleasure." His smile became a grin. "Now, you'd better get inside before you freeze."

Jenny turned and walked up the driveway, aware of him watching her every step of the way. She didn't look back until she reached the porch. Mitch was hardly more than a dark shadow. She waved and saw him lift his hand in return. The muffled roar of the bike's engine cut through the quiet night and then he was gone.

Despite the cold air, she waited on the porch until the sound of the bike faded completely. Only then did she turn and let herself inside. The big house was silent. Her mother was probably asleep. Stephanie Monroe was not the type to wait up worrying over her daughter. Her father would either be asleep in his own room or he might still be at the factory.

Either way, there was no one to question the condition of her clothes or the bruises starting to show on her arms. Tiredly Jenny climbed the stairs to her room. Turning on only the small lamp next to the bed, she stripped off the ruined dress and dropped it into the trash.

Moving over to the vanity table, she picked up a brush and started to drag it through her tangled hair. But she'd only completed a few strokes when she stopped and stared at her reflection in the mirror. Her lower lip was slightly swollen and tender to the touch, a legacy of Brad's brutality.

But it wasn't Brad she was thinking of as she touched her fingers gently to her mouth. *Just to remind you that it isn't always nasty.* It had apparently been an effective reminder, because she wasn't thinking of how close she'd come to rape. Instead, she was wondering what it would feel like to have Mitch Sullivan really kiss her.

Chapter 2

"So, what happened between you and Brad?" Beth Dryden leaned across the picnic table, her hazel eyes bright with curiosity.

"We broke up." Jenny shrugged, as if there were nothing more to be said.

"*That* much I gathered." Beth's tone was heavily sarcastic. "What I don't know is what happened. Did you finally figure out what a pompous jerk he is?"

She was tearing open her lunch sack as she spoke, taking out a lopsided peanut-butter-and-jelly sandwich. Beth's mother made sack lunches for all five of her children every morning. They were cheap and hastily made, but Jenny envied Beth the love that went into their preparation. Her own lunch was a delicately seasoned pasta salad and a chunk of home-made crusty bread, both prepared by the cook, who left the sack on a table in the foyer for her every morning.

"Earth to Jenny. Are you still in there?" Beth waved a hand in front of Jenny's face.

"Sorry." Jenny shook her head and smiled at her friend. "I was just thinking."

"Did you and your mom quarrel again?" Beth's guess was based on past experience. She'd known Jenny since kindergarten, and she'd learned to recognize the signs of Stephanie Monroe's sharp tongue.

"Yeah." Jenny sighed and put down her fork, giving up even the pretense of eating. Beth was the one person she could talk to without having to choose her words carefully. "She's furious with me for breaking up with Brad."

"Well, she's the only one. The guy's a creep. I told you that when you first started dating him," Beth reminded her, looking just a little smug.

"Well, you were right."

"So, what happened?" Beth abandoned her sandwich and leaned her arms on the table, fixing her friend with interested eyes. "Nothing happens in this town for months and then I go away for one lousy weekend to visit my aunt and the course of life as we know it shifts. Mary Jo Clayton grabbed me in the hall this morning before homeroom and demanded to know what was going on with you and Mr. Macho."

"What did you tell her?" Jenny reached across the table to snitch a chocolate chip cookie.

"I told her it was none of her business. What else could I say? I'm your best friend. I couldn't tell her I didn't know what she was talking about. And I'd like

to point out that I *still* don't know what happened."
Beth fixed Jenny with a look that was at once re-
proachful and demanding.

"After Sue's party Friday night, Brad decided that
I ought to prove how grateful I was for the honor of
going out with him. Things got a little ugly." The flat
sentence hardly began to describe those terrifying
minutes when she'd struggled with Brad.

"I hope you blacked his eye for him and then told
him where to get off."

"Not exactly. I had a little help, actually." Absently Jenny reached for half of Beth's sandwich.
"You'll never guess who came to my rescue."

"Who?" Beth slid the rest of her lunch across the
table and took Jenny's salad in trade. She'd never understand how Jenny could prefer peanut butter and
jelly to the gourmet quality meals that her family's
cook prepared. She took a bite of pasta salad and had
to suppress a sigh of pleasure.

"Mitch Sullivan."

"*Who?*" Beth's voice rose on the word, drawing
curious looks from some of the other students who
were eating nearby. Jenny grinned, satisfied with the
impact of her announcement.

"You heard me." She bit into Beth's sandwich.

"Mitch Sullivan?" Beth lowered her voice to a
stunned whisper. "The Mitch Sullivan who works at
Eddie's? The one with the incredible blue eyes who's
all the time getting into trouble?"

"That's the one." Jenny took a swallow of soda.

"*He* came to your rescue? I thought he was the sort
of guy a girl needed to be rescued *from*. My dad says

he's a hell-raiser and that he's going to get himself killed in a barroom brawl one of these days.''

"Maybe." Jenny frowned at the remains of Beth's lunch. She'd never paid much attention when people said things about Mitch Sullivan in the past, figuring they were probably nothing more than the truth. But she found herself vaguely annoyed by Beth's words. "He was very nice to me."

"Nice?" Beth wrinkled her nose. "That's not a word I associate with Mitch Sullivan. Wild. Or dangerous. Exciting, maybe. But not nice."

"Well, he *was* nice," Jenny said stubbornly. "He made Brad leave me alone and then he took me home. And he said I was to let him know if Brad gave me any more trouble."

"From what Mary Jo said, Brad avoided you like the plague at Willy's Saturday night." Willy's was a pizza joint and one of the most popular places for the high school group to hang out.

"I think Mitch put the fear of God into him." Jenny's smile held a touch of malice. "Mitch told him that he ought to remember that there weren't very many eunuchs playing football these days."

"He didn't!" Beth's laughter made Jenny grin. She hadn't seen much humor in the situation at the time, but remembering Brad's bulging eyes and pale complexion, she had to admit to a certain humor in the image.

"I thought Brad was going to faint."

"Can you blame him?"

"No. But it served him right." Jenny's expression hardened as she thought of bruises that still marked her arms. "I'm almost sorry I didn't let Mitch beat him to a pulp."

Beth picked up the last chocolate chip cookie and broke a corner off it, her expression thoughtful. "It sounds like you got awfully cozy with Mitch Sullivan."

The bell rang, signaling the end of lunch hour and calling the students back to class. In the rush to dispose of the remains of their lunches and gather up their books for the next class, there was no time for Beth to pursue the question. They parted company in the hall outside Beth's class, promising to meet after school.

Cozy? Jenny rolled the word over in her mind as she walked to her next class. She couldn't say that they'd gotten *cozy*, exactly. But she had to admit that Mitch had lingered in her thoughts all weekend. In fact, she'd found herself thinking about him and that soft kiss he'd given her even more than she'd thought about Brad.

To remind you that it's not always nasty, he'd said. Well, he'd certainly done that. She slipped into her seat just as the final bell rang, but her thoughts remained on Mitch Sullivan.

Mitch adjusted the butterfly valve on the carburetor he was rebuilding. Parts were neatly arranged on the workbench in front of him. The mellow swing of Jimmy Dorsey's orchestra came from the cracked speaker hanging on the wall of the garage. Mitch hummed "I Remember You" as he settled another part into place.

Old Man Riker—the "Eddie" in Eddie's garage—
was the one who insisted on big band music. He
claimed rock and roll was rotting the brain of America's youth.

Mitch doubted that keeping the garage as an island
of swing in a sea of synthesizers was going to do much
to save the country's youth, but he didn't mind the
music. After a few weeks, he'd been willing to con-
cede that he liked Gene Krupa as much as he did Bruce
Springsteen.

"Hey, Sullivan!" Jake Freeman's voice boomed off
the cement walls. Mitch cursed as a tiny screw slipped
through his fingers to land inside the carburetor. Now
he was probably going to have to take the whole thing
apart again to find the damned screw. Or maybe he'd
make Jake take it apart. With his teeth.

"What?" He snarled the question as he turned from
the bench. Jake grinned at him from the doorway, his
teeth gleaming white against his dark skin.

"You've got a visitor."

From the way Jake raised his eyebrows, Mitch knew
it had to be a woman. The thought did nothing to improve his mood. It had to be Susan Davis. The woman
was determined to carve a notch with his name on it in
her bedpost. He was equally determined to keep his
name off her furniture. And he'd done everything but
draw her pictures to make that clear. Maybe he needed
a sketchbook.

Grabbing up a rag only slightly less grease-covered
than his hands, Mitch strode toward the front of the
garage with long strides, not bothering to hide his irritation.

But when he stepped out of the garage, it wasn't Susan Davis waiting for him, standing next to a bright blue ten-speed. He doubted Susan had been on a bike since she left grade school. Jenny Monroe. His steps slowed as he saw her. What the hell was Jenny Monroe doing here?

Jenny tried to conceal her nervousness as she watched Mitch approach. Somehow, she hadn't remembered him being quite so large. Nor had she expected him to look so intimidating. He'd been positively scowling when he came out of the garage. When he saw her, the scowl lightened—but not by much.

Her fingers tightened on the handlebar of her bike. Her stomach was jumping with nerves and she felt breathless, as if she'd just stepped onto the high-dive board at the pool. She'd hardly admitted that she was coming here, even when she'd turned her bike this way. Now that she was here, she almost wished she hadn't come.

Mitch stopped a couple of feet away and looked at her, his eyes cool. Jenny instantly forgot all the clever things she'd thought to say by way of greeting.

"Hi."

"Hi." He didn't add anything to the flat response but simply stood there, watching her and waiting.

Jenny felt a flare of annoyance that helped burn away some of her nervousness. Who did he think he was? Standing there like some kind of . . . of a pasha, waiting for one of his subjects to speak.

"I just wanted to stop by and say thank you," she said, proud to hear how casual she sounded.

"You said that the other night."

"I didn't know there was a limit on the number of times you could say it."

"No limit."

"Then you won't mind if I say it again. Thank you. I really appreciate what you did." There was a snap in her tone that made the words sound almost like a challenge.

"You're welcome." Mitch's mouth curved in a half smile that helped to smooth Jenny's ruffled feathers. "I'm glad I was there."

"Me, too." She shivered, feeling chilled despite the warmth of the sun. "I don't like to think about what could have happened. Brad was really out of control."

"Don't think about it," Mitch told her. "It's over and you came out of it pretty well."

"Thanks to you."

"Louderman give you any trouble since?"

"No. He's made it a point to avoid me."

"Good." Mitch tugged the greasy rag through his fingers, and Jenny found herself remembering how strong his hands had felt supporting her that night. Strong but gentle.

That memory was part of the reason she'd come here. She'd wanted to see if her memories of Friday night had any basis in reality. He'd seemed like a knight in shining armor. The image was in such contrast to everything she'd heard of him that she'd felt compelled to see him in daylight and see if he was anything like what she remembered.

"I think you put the fear of God in Brad," she said.

Mitch tried very hard not to notice how kissable her mouth looked when she smiled. Or when she didn't smile. To tell the truth, he doubted if there was a time when Jenny Monroe didn't look kissable.

"How old are you?" The abrupt question made her blink, but she answered easily enough.

"I'll be eighteen in a month. Why?"

"Just wondered."

Eighteen in a month. And he'd be twenty-six in October. Eight years. Might as well be eight hundred, he reminded himself. Even if she were older, she was still Willard Monroe's little girl and that was a gap bigger than any age difference.

"I've got to get back to work," he told her, looking impatient. "Was there anything else?"

The dismissal was unmistakable. Unmistakable and unexpected. Jenny stiffened, her smile dissolving. The annoyance she felt was rapidly becoming familiar. What was it with this guy? One minute he was looking at her as if he liked what he saw and the next he acted as if he couldn't wait to get rid of her.

"Nothing else," she said coolly. "I just wanted you to know that I really appreciated your help."

"Like I said, I'm glad I came along." Mitch hesitated and then, unable to help himself, he reached out to touch the bruise just visible where the sleeve of her shirt had slipped up on her arm. "Do you have many of these?"

"A few." Jenny tugged her sleeve down self-consciously. "I'm lucky that's all I have."

"Yeah." He seemed about to say something more and then changed his mind, his expression closing abruptly. "See you around."

"Yes. See you around." But she was talking to his back as he turned and walked into the garage. Jenny stayed where she was for a moment before swinging up onto her bike and leaving the parking lot.

Peddling down the street, she considered the meeting with Mitch. He hadn't been particularly welcoming. At least not if she only listened to what he said. But the look in his eyes hadn't matched the words that came out of his mouth.

Jenny knew, without vanity, that she was pretty. She'd even been told she was beautiful. If she'd ever considered letting such compliments turn her head, she had only to look at her mother as an example of what happened to a woman who believed that looks were of vital importance.

But she hadn't reached nearly eighteen without learning to recognize when a man found her attractive. And she was willing to bet her trust fund that Mitch Sullivan was *very* attracted to her. He might not like it. In fact, he might actually *hate* it, but the attraction was there.

The light at the corner of Second and Cedar turned red as she approached and she stopped her bike, bracing one sneaker-clad foot on the curb. Frowning at the traffic, Jenny let her thoughts linger on Mitch Sullivan and his reluctant attraction. A mutual attraction. Only she wasn't fighting it.

Given a chance, Mitch was going to do his best to forget all about her. Jenny's mouth curved in a secretive little smile as the light changed and she started across Cedar. She wasn't at all sure she wanted Mr. Sullivan to forget her.

"You've got a visitor, Mitch." Jake's deep voice was threaded with amusement. "I didn't know you moved in such high circles."

Mitch lifted his head out of the engine compartment of the Chevy he was working on and glared across the fender at his friend. Jake's tone told him who the visitor was without a name being mentioned.

"Tell her I'm not here," Mitch snapped.

"Since she's watching me talk to you, I don't think she's going to believe that." Jake looked past Mitch and smiled, raising his hand in a beckoning gesture. "I'll leave you two alone," he said, grinning at Mitch's nearly savage expression.

Recognizing that there was no way out of it, Mitch straightened away from the engine and turned to face his visitor. He almost groaned when he saw her. Dammit all! Was she *trying* to drive him crazy? He was having enough trouble keeping her out of his thoughts without her showing up looking like something out of a sailor's dream.

What was wrong with her? Didn't she own anything that covered her? Never mind that the temperature was hovering at seventy degrees and the sun was blazing down out of a cloudless Colorado sky. Never mind that half the town was probably wearing even less. He was only concerned with the girl standing in front of him, wearing a snug denim skirt that showed a considerable amount of leg. Topping off the skirt was a skinny little knit top in cherry red that clung to every soft curve. He found himself wondering if she was wearing a bra and wishing he had the right to find out.

Dragging his eyes upward, Mitch met her gaze and saw a certain feminine knowledge there that told him she knew exactly where his thoughts had been. And that his reaction had been just what she'd expected. And wanted.

A wave of pure, masculine anger washed over him. Composed of equal parts sexual frustration and irritation at his inability to ignore the sweet temptation she offered, it hardened in the pit of his stomach, making him want to punish her for showing him how fragile his control really was.

"Hi." Perhaps she sensed his sudden bad mood, because Jenny's greeting was tentative, her eyes revealing her uncertainty.

"Hi." Mitch's voice was flat, his expression unreadable in the shadowed garage. "What are you doing here?"

"I came to see you." She must have been expecting the question, because her answer came without hesitation.

"Why? You've already thanked me for helping you out a few days ago."

"I . . . I thought it might be nice if we got to know each other," she said.

That was another answer she'd practiced, he thought. But she hadn't expected it to be so hard to get out, he decided, watching the way her eyes skittered from his face.

"You thought it would be nice to get to know me," he said, his tone considering.

"Y...yes." She had to clear her throat and he could see that the color had come up in her cheeks.

Damn, but she was attractive! He'd never met a woman he wanted more. If she'd been a little older—and if she hadn't been a Monroe—he'd have taken her out and discovered what it was about her that seemed to have crept under his skin, allowing her to invade his dreams and distract his thoughts.

But she *wasn't* older and she *was* a Monroe. Her current fascination with him undoubtedly stemmed from curiosity about how the other half lived. She'd probably never known anyone so completely outside her social class. She was slumming and she wouldn't stop bugging him until she'd had a little of her curiosity satisfied. And he was in just the right mood to not only satisfy her curiosity, but also scare her a little. Teach her a lesson about mixing with lesser mortals.

Jenny watched uneasily as Mitch set down the socket wrench he'd been using and started toward her. This meeting wasn't going quite the way she'd planned. It had all seemed much simpler when she'd been thinking about it in bed last night.

"So, you want to get to know me," Mitch said. There was a sharpness in his husky voice that she didn't understand. "I suppose you're curious about how the other half lives."

"The other half?" Jenny eased back a little as he stopped in front of her. He suddenly looked much larger than she'd remembered, towering over her. And the big garage suddenly seemed awfully dark and isolated.

"The poorer classes," he clarified. "Those of us who don't have cooks and maids and gardeners."

"I don't know what you're talking about." She tried to step back, wanting to put some distance between them. But her retreat was blocked by the workbench. Mitch completed her entrapment by bracing his hands on the bench on either side of her.

Startled and uneasy, Jenny raised her eyes to his. He was looking at her as if he hated her, his eyes a winter-sky blue, cold and hard. She flinched as his hands left the bench to cup her face.

"If what you wanted was a quick roll in the hay, why didn't you say so?"

Jenny was too stunned to even try to turn her head away as he lowered his mouth to hers. Her eyes closed reflexively as his lips covered hers.

He made no concessions for her youth and inexperience. The kiss was hard demand, laced with an anger she didn't understand. She'd fantasized about what it might be like if he kissed her. But there was nothing of fantasy in this kiss. This wasn't the tender kiss of passion she'd imagined.

She didn't struggle. Despite the anger she tasted in his kiss, she wasn't afraid of Mitch. Instinctively she knew he'd never hurt her, at least not physically. She didn't respond in any way but simply endured the scornful kiss, her soul aching with confused hurt.

Feeling the softness of her mouth under his, Mitch struggled not to take the kiss from contempt to desire. She smelled like sunshine, a fresh contrast to the musty grease scent of the garage. Her skin was silky soft under his hands. He wanted to see if the skin under that annoyingly sexy little top was just as soft.

The lesson, he reminded himself. He was teaching her a lesson, not indulging his sexual fantasies. But if the lesson didn't end soon, the teacher was going to forget what he was doing. And he wouldn't be much better than Brad.

He lifted his mouth from hers slowly, fighting the urge to kiss her again, to show her just how much he wanted her. He had to remember that there was a purpose to this, a purpose beyond discovering that she tasted just as sweet as he'd imagined.

Her lashes lifted and she looked up at him. Mitch felt a sharp stab in his chest when he saw the hurt he'd dealt her. Tears swam in her eyes, turning the chocolate brown to pansy black. She looked like a wounded fawn, all pain and confusion.

"Damn." The word came out on a sigh. He felt the bitter anger drain away, leaving behind nothing but regret and a sure knowledge that he'd just behaved like a first-class bastard.

"Why are you so angry at me?" Jenny asked, her voice quivering on the edge of tears.

"I'm not angry at you." Mitch sighed again and pulled a bandanna out of his back pocket. Folding it to find a clean corner, he dabbed at a greasy fingerprint on her cheekbone.

"Then why did you kiss me like that?"

Staring down into her eyes, Mitch sought the right words to explain the anger he'd felt. But how could he explain to her that just looking at her made him hard? And that having her standing so close and yet so far out of reach was sweet torture?

"Because I'm a jerk," he said finally. "I'm a jerk and I took my bad temper out on you. I'm sorry." He brushed his thumb over her lower lip.

"It's okay." She blinked to banish the threatening tears, but one escaped to slip down her cheek. Without thinking, Mitch bent to kiss it from her face. He hesitated, his breath brushing over her skin, instinct warring with common sense. Instinct won.

"I seem to be doing this a lot lately," he muttered as his mouth hovered for an instant before settling gently over hers.

This kiss was everything the first had not been. Feeling the difference, Jenny's lips softened under his, her hands coming up to rest on his chest. Mitch's mouth was warm and firm, easing away the hurt he'd given her. *This* was what she'd sensed a kiss could be. *This* was what had drawn her back, despite the way he'd dismissed her the day before. She sighed, her fingers flexing against the heavy cotton of his shirt as her lips parted beneath his.

It took all Mitch's willpower to resist the sweet invitation she offered. It would have been easy to forget all the reasons why he shouldn't kiss her. Feeling as if he were turning his back on the gates of paradise, he drew back, forcing himself to ignore the way her lips seemed to cling to his.

"Just to remind you that it's not always nasty," he whispered huskily.

"Not nasty at all," she agreed with a smile so appealing he had to move away to keep himself from snatching her back into his arms.

"I think you'd better go," he said, hoping he didn't sound as reluctant as he felt.

"Can I come back?"

God, was she *trying* to drive him crazy? His fingers curled into his palms as he shook his head.

"I don't think that's a good idea."

"Why not?"

"Why not?" He stared at her, wondering if it was possible she'd been sent to punish him for his sins. "Because I'm who I am and you're who you are."

"And never the twain shall meet?" she finished, lifting her eyebrows. The expression made her look just haughty enough for him to want to kiss it from her face.

"That's right," he said, moving a little further away from temptation.

"So you don't think we could be friends?"

Friends? It wasn't a desire for friendship that had him hard and aching.

"No, I don't think we can be friends," he said, making his tone harsh.

She frowned, looking at him as if he presented a particularly knotty problem. Mitch braced himself for more arguments.

"All right." Jenny nodded as if to emphasize her agreement. She thrust out her hand.

"All right?" He took her hand automatically, his fingers swallowing hers.

"Sure. You've obviously made up your mind. I'm not going to argue with you."

"Good." His tone lacked conviction so he repeated the word for emphasis. "Good."

"Well, it was nice seeing you again," Jenny said, as if they'd just shared a casual chat.

"Yeah. Same here." Mitch followed her to the front of the garage, lifting his hand in response to her casual wave as she got on her bike and turned it into the street.

"Jailbait, man." Jake's voice held real concern as he came to stand beside Mitch. "You know who her daddy is?"

"I know who he is." Mitch's eyes were on Jenny's slender figure and he didn't look away until she turned a corner and was out of sight.

"You know what you're doing?" Jake asked.

"I'm not doing anything." Mitch shrugged as he walked back to the job Jenny's arrival had interrupted.

"It looked like something to me." Jake followed him into the garage.

"Since when did you start spying on your friends?" Mitch asked without heat.

"Since my friends stated playing with fire. Besides, it was a little hard to miss when the two of you were standing in plain sight."

"You could have closed your eyes." Mitch picked up the socket wrench and leaned over the engine.

"I'll keep that in mind next time."

"There isn't going to be a next time. She's not coming back." Mitch gave him the reassurance he wanted, wishing the words didn't taste quite so bitter.

He was glad Jenny Monroe wasn't going to be coming around again.

And pigs had wings.

Chapter 3

As it happened, it really didn't matter whether he was glad, any more than it mattered whether or not pigs had wings.

The day after Mitch put Ms. Genevieve Monroe from his life for good, she showed up at the garage again.

Jake had taken a car for a drive to test a new brake job, so Mitch was working alone. With the Andrews Sisters singing about rum and Coca-Cola and the valve job going better than he'd hoped, Mitch was as content with the world as it was in his nature to be. At least until he heard that voice.

"Hi."

Without giving any consideration to his position, he jerked upright, cracking his head painfully hard on the raised hood. The jolt startled an oath from him. Or maybe it was the realization of who was standing behind him. One hand pressed to the back of his head, Mitch spun to face his visitor, his eyes expressing his disbelief at seeing Jenny standing there.

"What are you doing here?" He was beyond tact.

"I'm sorry. I know you probably didn't expect to see me." Her expression was penitent.

"No, I didn't. I thought we agreed that it wasn't a good idea for you to come here."

"Well, actually *you* agreed," she pointed out with scrupulous honesty. "And I wouldn't have come back," she continued before he could interrupt. "But I've got a flat tire."

"A flat tire." Mitch stared at her, but there was nothing other than innocence in her expression.

"Do you think you could change it for me?"

"The tire." Mitch nodded, feeling as if he ought to say no but unable to think of an excuse to do so. There was something wrong with this whole picture. He *knew* she hadn't come here just to have him change a tire for her. On the other hand, he was going to look like a fool if he accused her of letting the air out of her own tire just so she could show up here and remind him of what he'd turned away. As if he needed a reminder, he thought.

"If it's a problem, I guess I could call a tow truck," Jenny said slowly. Her forehead pleated in a concerned little frown.

"No. It's not a problem." Mitch wiped his hands on a rag as he followed her out into the parking lot.

Now, her clothes—*that* was a problem. Despite his determination not to let her get under his skin, Mitch couldn't prevent his eyes from lingering on the way her jeans molded her hips. Hips that swayed in a feminine invitation as old as time. Gritting his teeth, Mitch forced his gaze from that invitation, focusing instead on the car she'd stopped beside.

"What happened to the bicycle?" It was a silly question, but he needed something to distract him from noticing how nicely she filled out a T-shirt.

"I'm supposed to pick up some things for the housekeeper," she said. "You can't carry much on a bike."

"Not much," he agreed. *The housekeeper. Think about the housekeeper, Sullivan. Remember just how big a gap there is between you and Willard Monroe's little girl.*

"Any idea what happened to the tire?" *Besides the fact that you let the air out, of course.*

"I don't know what happened. It just went flat." Jenny shrugged. "I don't know much about cars, but I know better than to drive very far with a flat tire. This was the closest place so I came here. I hope you don't mind."

"Why should I? This *is* a garage." Mitch's tone was impersonal as he knelt beside the sadly deflated tire.

Like hell she didn't know what happened, he thought sourly. Even a total idiot knew how to let the air out of a tire. And she must think he was an idiot if she thought he wouldn't know what she was up to. He shouldn't have softened his treatment of her yesterday. He should have scared her out of her designer jeans and sent her on her way, convinced that he was just as dangerous as his reputation said he was.

Jenny hovered nearby as he jacked up the car and removed the tire. She didn't try to talk to him, but that didn't make her any less of a distraction. Mitch found himself aware of her every move. The more he tried to pretend that she wasn't there, the more he noticed her. By the time he got the tire off, his mood hovered perilously close to murderous.

"I'll just put it in the water tank and see if we can figure out what's wrong with it." He gave her a dangerous smile, waiting to gauge her reaction to that piece of news. But instead of looking nervous about being found out, Jenny looked curious.

"How will a water tank show that?" She followed him to the galvanized tub, watching as he lifted the tire and set it in the water.

"If there's a hole, I'll be able to see bubbles coming up from it. *If* there's a hole," he added with heavy emphasis. He gave her a sharp look, expecting to see guilt and embarrassment, but Jenny's attention was all for the tire.

"Oh, look! There's some bubbles. Is that what you mean?"

Mitch jerked his attention back to the half-submerged tire, his eyes widening as he saw the slow stream of bubbles appearing on the surface of the water. He began turning the tire and scooping water over it until he'd located the source of the leak.

And it definitely was a leak. A nail puncture from the look of it. Certainly more than enough to explain a flat tire. While he wouldn't put it past her to let the air out of her tire, he couldn't quite picture her jabbing nails into it. Obviously her explanation of how she'd come to be here had been nothing more than the truth. So much for overinflated egos, he thought, staring at the hole. He'd been so sure...

"Is that it?" Jenny leaned forward to inspect the damage, her hair brushing against his arm, her scent drifting up to him.

"That's it." Mitch yanked the tire from the tub too quickly, splashing water out of it and onto his shoes. Wet socks were a small price to pay for putting a little distance between himself and temptation.

"Can you fix it?" Jenny followed him into the garage.

It was rather like being on a strict diet and having the world's most delicious layer cake following you around, Mitch decided. "I can patch it."

"Good." She settled on a stool and fixed bright eyes on him. "You don't mind if I watch, do you?"

"No." *Why should he mind? She only made it difficult to remember his own name, let alone how to repair the tire.*

Later Mitch was convinced he must have set some sort of speed record for patching a tire. He tightened the last lug nut and settled the hubcap back into place, stifling a sigh of relief.

"What do I owe you?"

"Nothing." He wiped his hands on a rag and waved away her attempt to pay him. By now, he'd have cheerfully paid her—if she'd just go away and let him try to regain his peace of mind.

"Well, thanks, then." She hesitated, leaning against the open door. "Are you sure I can't pay you?"

"No. Really. Don't worry about it." Mitch backed away, his smile growing slightly strained around the edges. "Just try to keep your tires away from sharp objects from now on."

"I'll try." Jenny lifted her hand in farewell and slid into the little compact. She waved to Jake who was pulling into the parking lot as she was leaving.

Jake parked the car and got out. Coming to stand next to Mitch, he followed his friend's gaze to where Jenny's car was just disappearing.

"I thought she wasn't coming back," he said, sounding mildly surprised.

"She's not." Mitch turned and stalked into the garage, leaving Jake to stare after him with raised brows.

"I don't know, Jenny. Don't you think this is a little risky?" Beth frowned, her hazel eyes worried.

"Not particularly." Jenny dipped a French fry in catsup and popped it into her mouth. "It's not like I'm doing anything illegal or anything."

"No, but considering Mitch Sullivan's reputation, wouldn't you rather rob a bank?"

Around them, Bernie's Café bustled with customers. The sign out front proclaimed the best hamburgers in the world, and while *that* claim may have been a little grandiose, most people agreed that Bernie's burgers were the best in Ransome.

Jenny and Beth weren't paying much attention to the food at the moment. Though they'd graduated from Ransome High just a few weeks before, both were taking extra courses in summer school, prepar-

ing for college in the fall. Bernie's was a convenient
place to stop after school.

Jenny grinned at her friend. "Don't be such a
goose, Beth. I don't think Mitch Sullivan is nearly as
bad as people say. You know how people like to gossip."

"I suppose he couldn't have done *all* the things he's
blamed for," Beth agreed. "But where there's smoke
there's fire and there's an awful lot of smoke around
Mitch Sullivan." Beth stirred a spoon through her
milk shake, her expression still worried.

"I didn't say he was a saint." Jenny pushed her half-
eaten hamburger aside and reached for her soda. "I
just don't think he's all that bad."

"Fine. But that doesn't mean he's all that good, either." Beth shook her head. "I don't understand why
you're so determined to get him to notice you. I mean,
the guy's attractive and all—"

"Attractive?" Jenny interrupted incredulously.
"He's gorgeous!"

"All right. He's gorgeous." Beth conceded the point
reluctantly. "But he's also around twenty-five, if he's
a day. Don't you think he's a little old for you."

"I like older men," Jenny said stubbornly.

"Since when?"

"Since I met Mitch Sullivan."

Beth sank back against the red vinyl booth and eyed
her friend with exasperation. "You're biting off more
than you can chew," she said bluntly.

"But I'll certainly have a lot of fun trying," Jenny
said with a wicked grin.

"Genevieve Monroe!" Beth's expression was just as shocked as Jenny had expected. "You sound like you're actually thinking about ... about sleeping with this guy." Her voice dropped to a whisper. "You wouldn't, would you?"

"He hasn't asked me," Jenny said casually.

"But you wouldn't if he did, would you? We always swore we were going to wait until we were really, really in love before we went all the way."

"I hardly know the guy, yet. How do I know what's going to happen?" Jenny shoved her drink away impatiently.

"What I don't understand is why you're going to all this trouble to *get* to know the guy. You could date practically any guy in our class. What about Dave Larsen? He's gorgeous *and* he's nice and he's been trying to get you to go out with him since eighth grade. Why are you so set on Mitch Sullivan? I mean, he told you not to come back, didn't he?"

"That's not what his eyes were saying."

"His eyes?" Beth's tone suggested that Jenny might be in need of some serious professional help. "You're making up excuses to see him because you think *his eyes* said something?"

"You had to be there."

"You ran over a nail so you'd have an excuse to go back to the garage. Because you think he didn't mean it when he told you to get lost."

"He didn't tell me to get lost," Jenny protested.

"He told you not to come back again, didn't he?"

Jenny stirred restlessly, wishing she could make her friend understand. Of course, if she told Beth about the way he'd kissed her, about the way he'd brushed the tears from her face, it might make more sense. If she could make Beth understand how she'd felt, as if her whole life had been leading up to that one moment, maybe she could make her see what it was that was pulling her back.

But for some reason, she didn't want to share those moments, not even with Beth, who'd been her best friend all her life. She'd always shared everything with Beth. But this was something she couldn't share.

"You're making a big deal out of nothing," she said finally. She reached for the bill for their meal. "It's not like I'm going to kidnap the man. I'm just going to hang around a little and see what happens."

"Well, I think you're playing way out of your league." Beth pushed money across the table for her portion of the bill. "Look what almost happened with Brad. And I don't think he's half as dangerous as Mitch Sullivan."

"It was Mitch who rescued me," Jenny said stubbornly. "I don't think he's likely to turn around and attack me himself."

"There's dangerous and then there's dangerous," Beth muttered as she slid out of the booth.

"Stop sounding like the voice of doom." Jenny turned as they stepped out of Bernie's and grinned at her friend. "Come home with me and help me decide what to wear when I go by the garage tomorrow."

"You're not going back tomorrow!" Beth stopped in the middle of the sidewalk and stared at her as if she'd lost her mind. "You were just there yesterday."

"Well, I don't want him to forget me." Still grinning, Jenny grabbed Beth's arm and tugged her out of the path of a mother pushing a stroller.

"Forget you! The guy's more likely to have you arrested for harassment." But she allowed herself to be led toward Jenny's car.

"What's your excuse this time?" she asked after Jenny had pulled into the street.

"I thought I'd ask him if he wants to buy some raffle tickets." Jenny flipped on her right signal and shot Beth a quick look as she turned onto Magnolia.

"Raffle tickets?" Beth's voice rose on a disbelieving note. "You're going to ask him to buy raffle tickets for the new bleachers?"

"It's a very good cause," Jenny said virtuously.

"Jenny, they're raffling off a *quilt*. You're going to ask Mitchell Sullivan to buy tickets to win a *quilt?*"

"It's a very nice quilt."

"You're completely crazy." Beth sounded more resigned than upset. "You're stark raving mad." She contemplated the sad truth of that for a moment before her lips began to twitch. "I'd give just about anything to see the expression on Mrs. Potter's face when she announced that Mitch Sullivan held the winning ticket." She giggled. "I'd give almost as much to see his face when you ask him to buy a ticket."

"A raffle ticket?" Mitch repeated the words to make sure he hadn't imagined them.

"It's for a very good cause," Jenny said, looking anxiously up at him. "The school really needs new bleachers and you know how tight money is these days. The school board just can't approve that much for something that isn't absolutely essential.''

"Raffle tickets," he said again. "For a quilt."

"It's a really beautiful quilt," she assured him. "It's a red-and-green appliqué. It would be great for Christmas."

Mitch stared at her. She had to be kidding. He didn't know appliqué from appendix but he did know that he was the last person to need or want a quilt for Christmastime. Where did she think he was going to put it? It would look a little out of place in the converted shed where he was living now. Of course, he could probably hang it up to cover the worst of the cracks in the wall, keep out the cold next winter, but he doubted that was what she had in mind.

"I don't need a quilt," he said finally. Glancing up, he caught Jake's eyes on them. The other man grinned in response to Mitch's glare, cocking his head in Jenny's direction, as if to remind Mitch that this was the second time he'd been wrong about her returning. As if he needed reminding, Mitch thought in exasperation.

"Well, you could buy a couple of tickets anyway. They're only twenty-five cents each. Or you could get five for a dollar. Chances are, you won't win anyway. I mean, everybody in town is buying tickets. Mrs. Pomeroy is so determined to win it that she's bought thirty dollars' worth."

"So why should I buy a ticket if there's no chance of winning?" he asked, puzzled by her method of persuasion.

"I didn't say there was *no* chance. Besides, it's for a good cause. Don't you think it would be nice if we had new bleachers?"

Did she really think he gave a damn about whether or not Ransome High got new bleachers? He'd spent the most miserable years of his life incarcerated in that place. If it were reduced to rubble tomorrow, he wouldn't have felt a single pang of regret.

On the other hand, she was standing there, those big brown eyes expectant. He found himself reluctant to tell her just how little he cared about the bleachers. Or about anything else to do with the high school. Besides, if he bought some of the stupid tickets, maybe she'd go away. And stay away this time.

"Here. Give me two dollars' worth." He pulled a pair of crumpled bills out of his pocket and handed them to her. He was rewarded with a beaming smile that made him want to snatch her up and kiss her breathless.

"Thank you." Jenny held out ten tickets. Mitch took them from her, careful not to touch her fingers. His willpower was starting to fray around the edges. Even a light touch might be enough to make him forget all the reasons there were to keep his distance from Jenny Monroe.

A few minutes later, he watched Jenny peddle out of the parking lot. Why was it that he'd never noticed just how sexy a woman looked riding a bike?

"Good thing you made it clear that she wasn't to come back," Jake said from right behind him.

"Shut up. I don't want to hear another word about her."

"I ain't saying a word, man." But his grin said a great deal.

Mitch stuffed the tickets into his pocket and stalked into the garage. *This* time, she wasn't coming back. He was sure of it.

"Got a visitor, Mitch." Jake's voice was rich with amusement. He didn't have to say who the visitor was.

"No." Mitch groaned and braced his hands on the worktable, his head hanging in defeat. "What did I do to deserve this?"

"Just lucky, I guess." Jake didn't sound in the least sympathetic.

"I told her not to come back."

"Maybe you didn't sound like you meant it."

Mitch had to acknowledge that there might be some truth in Jake's words. Maybe he *hadn't* sounded like he meant it. If he were forced to be honest with himself, he didn't really want her to stay away. He'd even been half anticipating this visit.

But what he wanted and what he could have were two different things. He'd learned early in life that what a person wanted was sometimes the very thing that could hurt them. He'd had that lesson driven home when he'd seen his father beg for a drink, even while he lay dying of alcoholism. So no matter how attractive Jenny was, she had to go away and *stay* away. *This* time he'd make that clear.

He strode out of the garage, determined to put an end to this little game they were playing. For her sake, as well as his own, he had to make her understand that there could be no relationship between them.

Jenny was waiting for him, standing next to her bike, which just happened to have a flat tire.

"I'm sorry to bother you again," she said before he could say anything. "I know you didn't want me to come back here, but I just happened to be nearby when my tire started to go flat."

She gave him a look of such wide-eyed innocence that Mitch wanted to laugh. This time, she wasn't even really trying to pretend that there was no ulterior motive behind her presence. She knew exactly what she was doing to him, damn her beautiful eyes.

Jenny gasped in surprise when, without saying a word, he reached out and took hold of her wrist and began pulling her toward the garage. His hold was not harsh, but it didn't allow any room for argument, even if she'd had one to give.

He pushed open a door marked Office and led her inside, releasing her wrist as he shut the door behind them. Jenny had only a moment to notice an old leather sofa, its seat shiny with age and use, a stack of magazines on a scuffed table, and a battered coffeepot. A large and shabby wooden desk filled almost half the room, its surface covered with stacks of papers. It was a distinctly masculine room.

"You've got to stop doing this." Mitch's words drew her attention back to him.

"Doing what?" She widened her eyes in a way she knew made them look particularly attractive.

"Coming here," he said bluntly. "You've got to stop coming here with all these trumped-up excuses."

"Excuses?" She managed a touch of indignation. "It's not my fault my tire is flat," she lied without a blink.

"Isn't it? And I suppose it wasn't your fault that you came here to sell those raffle tickets yesterday?"

"That was for a good cause," she said self-righteously.

"And the flat tire on your car two days before that?"

"It's been a bad week for tires."

"It's been a bad week for foolish little girls to be poking their noses in places they don't belong."

"I don't know what you mean." But it was getting harder to keep up the injured-innocent act. Really, when he laid everything out like that, it was difficult to pretend it had all been a series of coincidences.

"You've got to stop coming around here like this, Jenny." He couldn't put it any more bluntly than that, he thought. Surely that would put an end to it.

"Why?"

"Why?"

"Yes, why?" She raised her chin in a way that made him notice the slender length of her throat. "Why do I have to stop coming around here? Don't you like me?"

"Like you?" Mitch stared at her, as he thrust his fingers through his hair. More than ever he was convinced that this was some punishment being meted out by a cosmic force. On one of the few occasions in his largely misspent life that he was trying to do the *right* thing, he was being presented with more stumbling blocks than he'd ever encountered when doing the *wrong* thing.

"The only reason I shouldn't come around is if you don't like me," Jenny said, making it sound like the most obvious thing in the world.

"Fine. I don't like you." It was nearly the truth. "Like" didn't begin to describe what she made him feel.

"I don't believe you," she returned promptly.

"What?" Mitch stared at her disbelievingly. "You just said that, if I didn't like you, you'd stop coming around."

"But I don't believe you don't like me."

"Why not?"

"Because you don't look at me like you don't like me."

"God help me." The words were as close to a prayer as Mitch had managed in years. He thrust his fingers through his hair again and looked around the untidy little room as if seeking divine guidance.

Reluctantly his gaze was drawn back to the girl standing in front of him. She was looking at him with her chin lifted stubbornly. But her eyes said that she wasn't at all sure. It was that vulnerability that made it impossible for him to be harsh with her. It was that same vulnerability that had had him kissing away the tears he'd caused a few days ago.

"Look, I'm not the sort of person you should know," he said finally. "Ask anyone in this town. They'll tell you I'm no good. I'm a troublemaker. A hell-raiser. I've been arrested more than once. Chances are I'll be arrested again. I'm the sort of person a girl like you ought *not* to know.''

"Most people would think that Brad Louderman is just the sort of person I *ought* to know," Jenny said, to no one in particular.

Mitch almost groaned aloud. Dammit all! How was he supposed to argue with that one?

"The only reason you're attracted to me is because you know you shouldn't be," he said finally.

"Is that the only reason you're attracted to me?" The color that rose in her cheeks belied her bold question.

"Whether or not I'm attracted to you is not the point." Mitch seemed to be having an increasingly difficult time remembering the point. He was losing the battle and he knew it. It was tough to fight a war you didn't wholeheartedly want to win.

"Couldn't we just be friends?" Jenny asked, shifting the argument subtly.

"Friends?" He looked at her, wondering how she'd managed to throw him so completely off stride that he was willing to even consider such a ridiculous idea. "What are your parents going to say about you being friends with someone like me?"

"I don't see any reason to ask them. Come on, Mitch." She gave him a coaxing smile. "You can't ever have too many friends."

Maybe not, but he also knew that some friendships could be dangerous. Looking at Jenny's soft mouth, what he felt wasn't friendship. Desire. Hunger. Need. Lust. Call it what you would, it *wasn't* friendship. On the other hand, he couldn't deny that he liked her. She was hard *not* to like.

"All right." He sighed and gave in. "But it's never going to work."

"Don't be so negative," she chided, grinning. "It's not all that hard to be friends with someone, you know."

Mitch looked at her, wondering if he was out of his mind. Friendship with Jenny Monroe? Who was he kidding?

Chapter 4

It was safe enough to agree to a friendship, Mitch told himself. It probably wouldn't take more than a week or so for Jenny to lose interest. At the moment, he was something new and different. He was older than the boys she'd gone to school with, and his reputation as a troublemaker probably made him seem all the more exciting.

He had enough experience to recognize sexual curiosity when he saw it. All he had to do was show her how boring he really was. Jenny Monroe was at an age where she was starting to feel her way as a woman—to flex her feminine muscles, so to speak. He just wished that she hadn't decided to do her flexing in his direction.

If he'd held a half-formed thought that, having gotten him to agree that she could come around, she might not bother to do so, Jenny proved him wrong almost immediately.

She showed up at the garage the next day.

"I'm busy," Mitch said, trying to sound discouraging.

"That's okay. I'll just watch you work." Jenny shoved an old stool next to the workbench and perched on it.

"You'll be bored," he warned. He had to drag his eyes from the smooth length of thigh left bare by her shorts. Didn't the girl own anything knee-length?

"No, I won't. Will it bother you if I watch?"

Bother him? Her presence was enough to *bother* him.

"It doesn't matter to me." He shrugged to show how little it mattered. "Seems to me you'd have something better to do than sit in a musty garage on a beautiful summer day."

"Like maybe play with my friends in the sandbox?" Her tone was sweetly sarcastic and Mitch threw her a startled look, reading the annoyance in her eyes. "I'm not *that* much younger than you are, Mitch. I'll be eighteen in less than a month. Past the age of consent for most things."

"Sorry." He gave her a half smile. "Eighteen seems pretty young to me."

"I'm sure it does. At your advanced age, it must be difficult for you to remember that far back." She nodded in mock understanding. "By the time I'm your age, I expect I'll be in a nursing home, just waiting for the grim reaper to come to call. Are you sure you don't want to sit down?"

"Okay, okay." Mitch lifted one hand, palm out in a sign of surrender. "I take it back. You're practically an old lady."

"Thank you." She grinned at him and he was helpless to do anything except grin back. Damn, but she was cute.

Friendship, he reminded himself, forcing his attention back to the job at hand. They'd agreed to a friendship. Nothing more.

"What are you doing?" Jenny leaned her forearms on the workbench and gave the assortment of parts an interested look.

"You're going to get greasy," Mitch warned her.

"I wash."

His mind immediately presented him with a vivid—and unwanted—image of her in the bath, her skin damp and flushed from the heat. He forced the image from his mind. Friendship, dammit. Friendship.

"So, what are you doing?" Jenny asked again.

"I'm rebuilding a master cylinder."

"Ooo, that sounds macho. Like something out of a kinky movie."

"It's part of the brakes," Mitch told her, hoping his repressive tone would discourage any more remarks about kinky movies. His imagination was active enough without her encouraging it. "Hand me that screwdriver, would you?"

Jenny handed him the tool and then leaned her elbows on the table and braced her chin in her hand to watch him work. It didn't take long before Mitch began to feel as if he'd just grown four thumbs on each hand. The only thing worse than having her talking to him and distracting him was having her quiet and distracting him.

"So, why are you selling tickets to raise money for new bleachers at the high school?" he asked, seizing the only topic that came to mind.

"Oh, it's the senior class gift to the school. You know, each senior class raises money for something the school needs. Didn't your class donate something?"

"If they did, no one asked me to sell raffle tickets for it," Mitch said, his tone dry.

"They were probably afraid you'd bite their head off. You can be rather intimidating, you know," she said, as if he might not have been aware of it.

"You don't seem particularly intimidated."

"I'm just more stubborn than most people," she said cheerfully.

And Mitch couldn't argue with that.

His prediction that she'd soon lose interest proved to be less than accurate—as had most of his predictions about Jenny Monroe. She dropped by the garage three or four times a week, usually after class. She didn't expect him to stop whatever he was doing to entertain her. She seemed content to watch him work, asking questions about what he was doing and handing him tools.

Mitch was reluctant to admit it, but he found himself looking forward to her visits. He'd never known anyone like her, and it wasn't just the gap between them socially that made her different. Or maybe it was. Maybe it was being born with the figurative silver spoon in her mouth that made Jenny so sure that life was going to turn out the way she wanted it to.

It wasn't that she was a Pollyanna, but there was a certain belief in her that, if she put her mind to it, most things were going to go her way. Just like the way she'd made up her mind to get to know him and she'd simply persisted until she wore down his resistance.

Not that he'd countered as hard as he should have, he admitted. His heart just hadn't been in it. Well, there was no real harm in letting her hang around. She seemed to enjoy poking around the garage, and he could almost manage to ignore her effect on his libido. Eventually she'd find another distraction and drift out of his life.

"So what do you think?" Jenny set the plate of cookies on the workbench, regarding them as proudly as a mother hen admiring her first chicks.

"They look great." Mitch gave the cookies an uneasy look. He was no expert on baking, but his nose suggested that they'd been in the oven longer than was ideal. "They're a little . . . brown, aren't they?"

"Yes. But they aren't really burned," she added quickly. "Just a little dark on the bottom, that's all. Try one. You too, Jake." She turned to include the other man in the invitation.

"Yeah. You too, Jake." Mitch's smile held friendly malice. "You like chocolate chip cookies, don't you?"

"Sure." When he saw the cookies, Jake looked as if he regretted his quick agreement, but there was no taking it back now. "Did you make these yourself, Jenny?"

"Mrs. Dryden helped me. She's teaching me to cook. Here." She pushed the plate toward Mitch.

Bowing to the inevitable, he picked up a cookie. His eyes cut to Jake, threatening future retribution. With an uneasy smile, Jake took a cookie. Satisfied that he wasn't stepping into the unknown alone, Mitch bit into his cookie. "Dark on the bottom" did not begin to describe the taste. They were "dark" all the way through, and the taste was somewhere between scorched and charred, with occasional bursts of chocolate from the chips.

Aware of Jenny's anxious eyes on him, Mitch chewed manfully and swallowed.

"They're great," he told her, swallowing again to get rid of the crumbs that didn't seem to want to go down. "They're really great."

"Yeah, Jenny. They're great." Jake added his enthusiasm to Mitch's.

"You really like them?" she asked, her smile bright enough to dazzle.

"I love them." Mitch put the rest of the cookie into his mouth without a second thought.

"Me, too. Can I take a few with me?" Jake managed to look hopeful and was rewarded by another smile.

"Sure." Jenny pushed the plate toward him, beaming with pleasure.

Mitch watched enviously as Jake took a handful of cookies and disappeared behind a Ford on the other side of the garage. There was a trash barrel over there, and he didn't doubt that the cookies had already been deposited into it.

"You want another one, Mitch?"

About as much as he wanted to eat a bolt.

"Thanks." He picked up a cookie and ate it, wondering why it should matter to him whether or not she thought he liked her cookies. "Is Mrs. Dryden your cook?"

"No. She's my best friend's mom." Jenny took a cookie and nibbled on the edge, seemingly oblivious to the scorched taste. "Mrs. Billings is our cook and she doesn't like having me in the kitchen. She doesn't like having *anyone* in the kitchen, actually."

"Does your mom do any of the cooking?" he asked. It occurred to him that he couldn't remember hearing her so much as mention her mother.

"*Mother?* In a kitchen?" The idea seemed to boggle her mind. "I doubt she'd set foot in one even if she were starving to death."

"She doesn't like to cook?" Mitch picked up a wrench and turned back to the car he'd been working on before Jenny's arrival.

"I don't think she's ever tried it. Mother doesn't do anything like that. You know, housework or gardening or cooking. I don't think I've ever seen her with her hands dirty."

Mitch thought of his own mother, of the way she'd worked to earn a living. He couldn't remember ever seeing her with her hands idle, not until she got sick; even bedridden, she'd insisted on doing mending.

"What does your mother do?" he asked, trying to imagine how she filled her time.

"Oh, lots of charity work." Jenny slid off her stool and came over to lean on the fender across from him, watching him work.

"I wouldn't think there'd be that much charity work to do in a town this size."

"She spends a lot of time in Denver." She picked up one of the worn spark plugs he'd removed and turned it over in her hands.

"You miss her?" Something in her tone had him making the words a question rather than a statement.

"Not particularly." She caught his quick look and shrugged. "We don't get along all that well. Actually, I'm not sure anyone gets along with my mother. She's . . . difficult."

"What about your father?"

"Oh, Daddy doesn't get along with her, either. He spends a lot of time at the factory. And he travels quite a bit, checking on suppliers and things." She leaned her forearms on the fender, her expression pensive. "I guess he could have someone else do that kind of thing, but I think he's just as glad to have an excuse to get out of the house."

Her candor left Mitch with no response. Her matter-of-fact tone made sympathy seem awkward. He turned his attention to the car, as if putting in new spark plugs took all his concentration. Maybe he should have paid more attention to all those aphorisms about not judging others. He'd assumed that a girl like Jenny Monroe would have a picture-book life. Money, loving parents, everything she could possibly want.

"What about your parents? What do they do?"

"They're dead," he said shortly.

"I'm sorry." She sounded distressed, as if she thought she'd brought up unpleasant memories.

"It was a long time ago," he said, shrugging. He reached for a spark plug wrench. "My dad was an alcoholic and he drank himself to death when I was twelve. My mother worked herself to death trying to keep a home together. She died when I was nineteen."

"How terrible for you."

Startled by the pain in her voice, Mitch looked up and felt his heart catch when he saw the shimmer of tears in her eyes.

"It was a long time ago," he said again, uncomfortable.

"But it must have hurt terribly, to be left alone so young."

"I guess." He looked away from the emotion in her eyes, uncertain of his response. He couldn't remember ever having someone shed tears over his pain. "I didn't see all that much of Mom. She worked so many hours."

"But she must have loved you very much, to have worked so hard for you."

"Yeah." He bent over the engine compartment again. There was no sense in trying to explain that he'd barely known his mother as anything other than a tired woman, old before her time, who'd rarely spoken, except to caution him against turning out like his father.

A pair of emotional orphans, he thought, looking at Jenny. She was arranging the old spark plugs in a neat row on the fender. The last place he'd expected to find a kindred spirit was in Jenny Monroe.

It was a shame she couldn't ever be anything more than that.

"Good morning, pumpkin." Willard Monroe smiled at his daughter as she entered the dining room.

"Daddy!" Jenny came around the table to kiss his cheek.

The warm spicy scent of his cologne teased her with childhood memories. She'd bought him a bottle of that cologne for Christmas the year she was six, using money her grandmother had given her. Her mother had sneered when she saw the bottle, commenting that Grandma Monroe should have known better than to trust a six-year-old's taste.

Jenny had been devastated, but her father had taken her on his lap and told her that *he* liked the cologne very much and hoped she would get him a bottle every Christmas. And she had, every year since. And he'd continued to wear it. She wondered if he remembered how the tradition had started.

"What are you doing home?" she asked as she sat down. She selected a muffin from the assortment piled on a plate in the center of the table.

"I'm just getting a late start this morning," he said.

"Oh." Jenny couldn't quite keep the disappointment out of her voice and he glanced up from folding the newspaper, his brown eyes questioning.

"Was there something you wanted to talk to me about?"

For a moment, she was tempted to say yes, but she caught the quick look he threw at his watch and shook her head.

"No. Nothing. I just thought I might get to have breakfast with my favorite father."

"You'll have to start getting up a little earlier, slugabed." His smile momentarily erased the tight lines around his mouth. He set the paper next to his plate before getting up. Coming around the table, he dropped a quick kiss on top of her head. "Have a good day, sweetheart."

"You too, Daddy." But she doubted he even heard her. Before he'd reached the door, his thoughts would have turned completely toward the day's tasks.

Jenny cut open her muffin and spread butter on its warm surfaces. Biting into it, she chewed and swallowed, tasting nothing. Pouring a cup of coffee from the silver carafe, she lifted it in a mocking salute to the empty room.

"Happy birthday, Genevieve Monroe. Happy eighteenth birthday."

She blinked back tears as she sipped the coffee.

Mitch looked up as Jenny came into the garage. He was relieved to see that her hands were empty. She'd gotten in the habit of sharing her latest culinary efforts with them once or twice a week. She was improving as a baker, but her offerings were still something to regard with caution.

"Hi."

"Hi." He stood up and reached for a rag to wipe the grease from his hands as he watched her approach.

She was wearing a bright pink halter dress that clung in all the right places and ended several inches above the knee. Mitch tried not to think that she reminded him of a particularly delicious strawberry lollipop. It was really too bad that a blizzard was unlikely in July. Maybe she'd look less edible in a snowsuit.

"No cookies?" he asked.

"No. Beth and her mom had to go to Cheyenne to see Beth's grandmother. Every summer, she announces that she's dying and wants to see her family before she goes. Since she's a zillion years old, they have to believe her and they all go rushing to her bedside."

"And she makes a miraculous recovery?" Mitch guessed.

"You got it. But she's a sweet old lady and she always throws a great party to celebrate her recovery so no one minds too much. There are some—cynical sorts—who suspect that she only announces she's dying as an excuse to throw the party."

She grinned up at him and Mitch had to swallow hard against the urge to haul her into his arms and kiss the smile from her mouth. This friendship thing was getting harder instead of easier. The more he got to know Jenny, the more he wanted her. He'd also come to like her, which made him reluctant to try to save his sanity by telling her to stay away.

"So, what have you got planned today?" He cleared his throat and turned away from her as he spoke.

"Nothing. I thought I'd hang out here for a little while, if you and Jake don't mind."

Mind? Why should he mind slow torture?

"Jake's got the day off."

"Well, then, I'll hang around for a while."

It was on the tip of his tongue to tell her that he was going to be terribly busy, but he made the mistake of turning to look at her first. There was that damned uncertainty in her eyes, that vulnerability that paralyzed his common sense.

"I don't mind," he heard himself saying. "I just assumed you'd have other things to do today."

"Like what?" She raised her eyebrows, puzzled.

"Don't people usually have other things to do on their eighteenth birthday," he asked, his half smile anticipating her surprise. She didn't disappoint him.

"How did you know it was my birthday?" she asked.

"I have my sources," he said mysteriously. "Happy birthday."

"Thanks." Her smile seemed forced, but Mitch told himself it was probably his imagination.

"So don't you have anything better to do than hang around here?" he questioned, his tone teasing.

"No."

The bald denial was not what he'd expected and it took him a moment to respond.

"No? Come on, what about your parents? Don't they have plans?"

"Yes. They just don't include me." Her smile was thin and failed to conceal the hurt she felt. "Mother is in Denver and I'm sure she'd rather not be reminded of my birthday. It's hard to tell people that you're thirty when you have a daughter who's eighteen," she said cynically.

"What about your father?"

"He forgot." Jenny's sigh quivered on the edge of breaking. "He's been so busy lately. I don't blame him for forgetting."

She might not blame him but Mitch didn't feel nearly as charitable. If Willard Monroe had been in front of him at that moment, he'd probably have been tempted to knock out a few of his teeth. But he couldn't say as much to Jenny.

"Well, I'm not busy. Happy birthday, Jenny."

"Thanks."

He hesitated a moment and then turned and slid a small package out from behind a tool chest on the bench.

"I got you a present," he said reluctantly.

"You did?" Jenny stared at the gaily wrapped box as if she couldn't believe what she was seeing.

"It's not much," he warned her as she began tearing at the ribbon. He was sorry now that the idea had ever occurred to him. What on earth could he buy for Genevieve Monroe that could compare to the things she already owned? But it was too late now. She had the wrapping off and was lifting the lid.

"Oh, Mitch, it's lovely," she breathed, looking at the heart-shaped silver locket nestled on a bed of cotton.

"It's nothing special," he said again.

"It's beautiful." She lifted it from the box, holding it up so that the light reflected from it. "I've never seen anything so pretty. Here. Help me put it on."

She handed him the chain and turned her back as she lifted her hair out of the way. Mitch immediately became all thumbs. The tiny latch had obviously been designed with something other than human fingers in mind—*male* fingers, anyway.

When he finally got it undone, he was confronted by the necessity of getting the chain around Jenny's neck, which meant getting much closer to her than was wise. Swallowing, he edged forward and reached around her to set the chain in place, which was not easy to do when he was trying to avoid touching her, even the smallest amount.

And then he had to bend close to her to work the latch. Close enough to catch the faint scent of soap and shampoo that lingered on her skin and hair. Surely the most erotic scent in the world, at least when it was on Jenny.

Why hadn't he bought her a knickknack of some kind? Something that didn't have to go on her person, something that didn't require his assistance.

"There." The word held a wealth of relief as the latch cooperated at last.

"How does it look?" Jenny released her hair, letting it tumble onto her shoulders as she spun to face him, her eyes expectant.

"It looks . . . fine." It was a lame answer, but it was the best he could come up with. To tell the truth, the sight of the locket lying against her skin made him want to replace it with his mouth.

"Fine? It's beautiful."

"Come on, you must have a ton of jewelry, all of it nicer than this."

"But I didn't get any of it for my birthday."

"Well, you must have gotten a lot of birthday presents that were more exciting."

"Daddy's lawyer has transferred a block of stock to my name every year since I turned twelve. And it's hard to wear a block of stock around your neck." She looked up at him, still fingering the locket. Her smile held a hint of tears. "Thank you, Mitch. Thank you so much."

Before he could respond, she rose up on her toes to brush a kiss across his mouth. At least, later, he thought that was all she'd intended. Just a quick kiss, a thank-you.

But she set her hands on his shoulders for balance, and his hands somehow came up to settle on the curve of her waist. And her mouth was lingering on his. And the kiss was suddenly anything but quick.

Mitch forgot all about the reasons he should be keeping her at a distance. He forgot about who she was and who he was and how old she was and every other argument he'd given himself about the complete unsuitability of their being together. He forgot everything but the way she felt in his arms, the taste of her on his mouth.

She tasted just as sweet as he remembered, her lips soft and welcoming, tempting him. His hands shifted, his arms circling her back to draw her closer. It seemed incredible that this was the first time he'd kissed her without trying to either comfort or discourage her. How could he possibly have resisted temptation as long as he had?

Jenny's hands slid into the thick black hair at the nape of his neck, her fingers kneading his scalp as she pressed herself closer to him. This was what she'd known could happen, what she'd sensed lay just out of reach when he'd kissed her before.

Her mouth parted to accept the bold possession of his tongue, and she felt her knees weaken as he claimed the territory she'd gladly surrendered. She'd been kissed before and she'd found it pleasant, even a little exciting. But she'd never experienced anything like this, never felt as if she wanted to just melt into another person.

She heard her own soft whimper of protest as Mitch dragged his mouth from hers. He heard it, too, and she felt the shudder that went through him as his hands dived into her hair, tilting her head as his mouth came down on hers again.

If she'd thought the first kiss powerful, this one was pure lightning. She was swept up on a wave of passion, her slender body like a reed bending before a flood.

Mitch kissed her as if he were starving and she offered the only hope of sustenance. For Jenny it was revelation. For Mitch it was the fulfillment of too many hours of fantasizing about her. Fantasies he'd sworn would never come true. A decision he'd made for good reason.

He pushed the thought aside. He didn't want to remember all the reasons he shouldn't be doing this. He didn't want to think of anything except how right she felt in his arms, her mouth all soft hunger under his. He wanted to pick her up and carry her into the office and lay her down on the old couch. He wanted to strip the soft little dress from her so that nothing lay between him and her silky skin.

The image was so vivid and his own reaction to it so powerful, it served to shock him into an awareness of what he was doing. And where it was leading.

Jenny felt bereft as Mitch dragged his mouth from hers. He leaned his forehead against hers as if he couldn't quite bring himself to move any further away. His breathing was loud in the quiet garage, and she could feel the tension in the hands that still lay against her back.

"Mitch?" She couldn't have said just what she was asking, only that she didn't want him to let her go. She didn't want him to ever let her go.

"This is not good," he said.

"It feels good to me." She blushed at her own boldness and lowered her eyes to where her fingers were toying with a button on his shirt.

"You know what I mean," he said, his voice husky. He caught her hand, stilling its movements. But he didn't pull it away from him. Instead, he pressed her palm flat against his chest. Jenny could feel the heavy rhythm of his heart beneath her fingers, as well as the strength of his hand holding her.

"I swore this wouldn't happen," he said, almost as if speaking to himself.

"I don't see what's so terrible about us kissing." She gathered her courage and lifted her eyes to his face. "I liked it."

He almost groaned aloud. How much torture was he expected to bear?

"I liked it, too. But that's not the point." He forced himself to take a step back, releasing her hand so that they weren't touching. "Friendship, remember? That's what we agreed to."

"But—"

"No buts, Jenny. If you want more than friendship, you're going to have to look somewhere else."

His tone was stern and the look in his eyes told her that he meant exactly what he said. Jenny reached up to finger the locket he'd given her, her eyes searching his face. But there was no give in him.

"All right, Mitch. Friendship. I won't ask anything else."

She was asking for a whole hell of a lot more than friendship, just standing there, he thought. Her hair was tousled where his fingers had combed through it, and her mouth was softly swollen from his kisses. It took every scrap of willpower he could hammer together to keep from reaching out and drawing her into his arms again.

"Good," was all he said.

Chapter 5

"**Y**ou're asking for trouble, Jenny. I can feel it in my bones. Mitch Sullivan is trouble with a capital *t*." Beth fixed her friend with a worried look.

"You're starting to sound like Robert Preston," Jenny said lightly. "But this is Ransome, not River City and Mitch isn't a pool table."

"Go ahead and laugh at me, if you want, Jenny, but you're playing with fire and you know it." Beth's tone was stiff, her expression hurt.

"I'm sorry, Beth." Jenny was instantly sorry that she'd dismissed her friend's concern so flippantly. "Don't worry, Beth. I know what I'm doing."

"Do you?" Beth was unconvinced. "He's so much older than you are, Jenny. And he's had a lot more experience."

Before Jenny could respond, they were interrupted by the loud buzzing of the kitchen timer.

"My cake!" Jenny leaped from her chair and snatched open the oven door, grabbing for a pot holder at the same time.

"Jeez, Jen, it's not going to burn if it's in the oven thirty seconds longer than the recipe says," Beth said, chuckling at her friend's burst of activity.

Jenny ignored her. She was determined not to burn this cake. Beth's mother had helped her with the preparation, but she'd had to leave to pick up her youngest child from preschool and she'd left Jenny to take it out on her own. And Jenny had no intention of failing.

She lifted the cake out of the oven and carried it gingerly to the waiting rack, handling it as if the pan contained nitroglycerin rather than a relatively sturdy pound cake.

"What do you think?" she asked as she set the cake down gently.

Beth left the chair she'd been slouched in and came over to look at the patient.

"I think it looks like a cake," she said at last. "It looks fine."

She shrugged, unable to understand why Jenny was so anxious to learn to cook. As far as Beth was concerned, it was a skill she could do without. If she couldn't cook, then her mother wouldn't have been able to ask her to handle dinner a couple of times a week.

"Don't think I've forgotten what we were discussing," she said.

"You mean what you were lecturing me about," Jenny said, slanting her an exasperated look. "Mitch isn't going to ravish me, Beth."

"The problem is, I'm not sure he'd *have* to ravish you," Beth shot back.

After setting the timer for five minutes so that she could turn the cake out at exactly the right moment, Jenny looked at Beth, her expression both irritated and understanding.

"If it will make you feel any better, Mitch has no intention of ravishing me, with or without my cooperation. He told me as much, in no uncertain terms."

She reached up to finger the silver locket she wore, remembering the way his body had said something else entirely.

Beth, reading her expression, did not look comforted. "I'd feel better if you told me that you didn't intend to ravish him," she said bluntly.

"Oh, come on. Do you think I'm going to throw him to the ground and have my wicked way with him?" Jenny's laughter emphasized the ridiculousness of the image.

"No. But in your own quiet way, you usually manage to get what you want, whether it's good for you or not."

Jenny shrugged and turned back to her cake. Beth was her best friend, but there were some things they just couldn't share. And the way she felt about Mitch was one of them.

Her main concern now was to convince Mitch that she didn't need him keeping his distance for her own good.

* * *

If it had been difficult for Mitch to keep his hands off Jenny before, it was twice as hard after the kiss they'd shared. He'd half hoped that she'd stay away after that, that she might have been frightened. But apparently it took more than a searingly erotic kiss to scare her, though it had damn sure been enough to scare him.

She came back to the garage two days later, and, from the way she acted, you'd never know anything had happened. Unless you counted the way she sometimes flushed if he happened to catch her eyes, or a certain awareness he sometimes seemed to see in her eyes.

If Jenny didn't feel a change, Mitch more than made up for it. He'd taken more cold showers in the week since that kiss than he had in the twenty-six years of life that had gone before it. He no longer had to imagine how it would feel to kiss her the way he'd kiss a woman he wanted. Now he knew. And knowing was infinitely worse than imagining. Before, he'd been able to console himself with the thought that forbidden fruit always looked sweeter. Now he knew that Jenny Monroe was every bit as sweet as he'd dreamed.

And just as forbidden as ever.

Distance, he told himself. That was what he needed. If she just didn't come around, reminding him of all he was trying to forget, maybe he could get it into perspective.

Which didn't explain at all how he came to hear himself inviting her to go on a Fourth of July picnic with him.

* * *

It was just that he hadn't wanted her to spend the holiday alone, the way she'd spent her birthday. When she'd mentioned that her parents were going to be in Denver for the weekend, he'd assumed she'd be spending the day with the Drydens.

"Beth invited me but I told her I couldn't. I just hate pushing myself in on family gatherings." She shrugged self-consciously. "That probably sounds dumb."

"No."

He wished it did. Instead, her words struck an answering chord that he couldn't ignore, no matter how much he wanted to do so. Jake had invited him to spend the day with his family and he'd turned him down, mumbling something about having other plans. He knew Jake's family and liked them. They seemed to like him. But they were still *Jake's* family, not his. And he'd decided not to push himself on them, the same way Jenny hadn't wanted to intrude on the Drydens.

It was stupid really. No doubt, they were both welcome at their friends' homes. But he understood how Jenny felt. And that was what had him opening his mouth and offering an invitation he'd no business issuing.

"Why don't we pick up something portable for supper and go up on Falune Hill and watch the fireworks from there?"

Jenny's head jerked up and she stared at him as if she couldn't believe what she'd heard. Mitch didn't blame her. He couldn't believe it, either. But the words were out and he could hardly take them back.

"I'd like that," she said slowly. "I could ask Mrs. Billings to make up a picnic for us."

"As long as it's not goose liver and petit fours," Mitch said.

"I'll make sure neither of those things are on the menu," she promised. She smiled, her eyes sparkling with pleasure. "This will be fun."

"Yeah. Fun." He couldn't help but return her smile, despite his misgivings.

He hoped *fun* was the right word, but he was afraid *dangerous* fit better.

Mrs. Billings provided them with a delicious and very traditional supper of fried chicken, potato salad and all the trimmings. By the time they got to the homemade apple turnovers, Mitch was complaining that he'd eaten so much he was going to die. But he managed to consume two turnovers before admitting defeat.

"Do you eat like this all the time?" he asked as they packed the leftovers away. "It's a wonder you don't weigh a ton."

"Usually, we have something a lot lighter. Mother is very careful about her weight, so dinner is usually broiled fish or chicken when she's home. And when she isn't, I usually just have a salad or a sandwich. I think Mrs. Billings enjoyed getting a chance to make something a little more traditional."

"Well, she certainly outdid herself." Mitch accepted the cup of coffee she'd poured from the thermos and leaned back on his elbows on the blanket they'd spread over the thick grass.

Falune Hill was really a foothill of the Rockies, a prelude to the peaks that lay behind them. During the winter, its smooth slope provided a favorite sledding spot. In the summer, it was an occasional make-out spot, but Mitch had guessed that, on the Fourth, most people would be in town celebrating. He'd guessed right and they had the hilltop to themselves.

"It looks so pretty from up here," Jenny said, looking at the town spread out beneath them. Lights were just starting to come on as the sun sank behind the mountains.

"The Black Hole of Calcutta probably looked pretty good from this angle," Mitch commented cynically.

"Ransome has its problems, but I don't think it can compete with the Black Hole of Calcutta." Jenny linked her arms around her knees, resting her cheek on them, as she looked at him. "If you dislike it so much, why do you stay?"

"Money." Mitch's answer was succinct.

"You could be a mechanic anywhere."

"I don't plan on being a mechanic for the rest of my life."

"What do you want to do?" she asked.

"See the world, I guess." He glanced at her and gave her a self-conscious smile. "Sounds stupid, I suppose. But I've always wanted to travel."

"Sounds great but it's tough to find a job that'll pay your way to see the world."

"Not if you're a writer."

"A writer?" It was the last answer she'd expected and she sat up, releasing her hold on her knees as she turned to look at him. "You want to write?"

"I already do," he admitted, surprising himself as much as her. The only person he'd ever mentioned his ambitions to was Jake, and even Jake didn't know that he'd actually sent things out.

"I've sold a few articles. Nothing spectacular, but enough to fool me into thinking it's possible to earn a living at it." He sat up, resting his elbow on his raised knee and staring at the town unseeingly. "I've got almost enough money saved to pay my way to Europe and to live for a few months, if I live dirt cheap."

"You're going to Europe?" Jenny fought to keep her voice neutral. Not for anything did she want him to know that his words had sent a sharp pain through her heart.

"That's the plan. I can send articles back to the States from Europe and still have time to work on a book."

"What kind of book?" Jenny was surprised to hear how normal her voice sounded. You couldn't tell her heart was breaking at all.

"I don't know yet." Mitch laughed and shrugged. "I'll figure it out when the time comes."

They were silent for a while, watching as more and more lights came on in the town. There'd be a big crowd gathering at the high school, waiting for full dark when the fireworks display would start. Jenny felt no regret at not being down there. She knew from experience that there was no lonelier place to be than in the midst of a crowd.

"What about you?" Mitch asked suddenly. "You're going to college this fall. What are you going to major in?"

"I'm not sure." College seemed impossibly far away. It was hard to remember how she'd looked forward to going, to leaving the polite tensions of her home behind at last. Since meeting Mitch, she'd hardly given school a thought.

"You must have something you want to do," Mitch prompted.

"Actually, I'd like to be a nurse," she admitted slowly. "When Grandma Monroe was in the hospital and she was dying, I watched the way the nurses treated her. They made it easier for her, and I thought that was what I'd like to do someday."

"Nothing wrong with nursing as a career."

"Not to hear my mother talk." Jenny's laugh held no humor. "She thinks it's a horrid idea and she hopes I'll give it up before I graduate."

"What do you think?"

"I think it won't hurt to have a college degree." She lifted one shoulder in a half shrug. "They'll still need nurses in four years. Oh, look! They're starting the fireworks."

Mitch obediently turned his attention to the display they'd come to watch. They had a terrific view from where they were, though distance made the fireworks seem smaller and softer somehow.

But the bursting lights didn't hold his attention for long. He found Jenny's face much more interesting.

She was as enthralled by the fireworks as a child, her eyes wide, her lips slightly parted as she watched.

How had she managed to get so far under his skin, he wondered. He'd certainly known women who were better looking. But he'd never met one who stirred him more. It wasn't simply knowing she was out of reach, that he shouldn't be within ten feet of her. It was something deeper and stronger than that. Something he wasn't at all sure he wanted to name.

"Did you see that one? Wasn't it beautiful?" Jenny turned her head to look at him, her words trailing off when she saw that he wasn't looking at the fireworks but was instead staring at her with an intensity that sent a shiver up her spine.

"Beautiful," he murmured, apparently in response to her comment. But Jenny didn't think he was talking about the fireworks and she felt her knees weaken.

"You're beautiful," he said, leaning closer.

Jenny watched him, her heart starting to pound. His hand came up to find the clip that held her hair back from her face. Soft golden curls tumbled forward and he caught a handful of them, weighing them as if they were spun of pure gold.

"You have the most beautiful hair," he said, speaking almost to himself.

Jenny swallowed hard but said nothing. She couldn't have uttered a word if her life depended on it. Even in the shadowy moonlight, she could feel the intensity of his gaze and it made her knees feel weak. Her tongue came out to wet lips that seemed suddenly very dry.

Mitch's gaze sharpened on the quick movement. He felt hunger pool hard and tight in the pit of his stomach. One kiss, he thought. One kiss could do no harm. He knew he was playing a dangerous game, had been when he suggested that the two of them come up here. Hell, he'd been on shaky ground from the moment they met, he admitted.

One kiss was hardly going to add much to the list of stupid things he'd done since she'd come into his life. Not that it would have mattered if it did, because he couldn't have stopped himself from taking it. She was watching him with eyes that revealed the same hunger he felt, and he could no more turn away from that look than he could have sprouted wings to fly from the hilltop.

Jenny's eyes drifted closed as he slid one hand deeper into her hair, drawing her into his kiss. This time, there was no gentle testing, no coaxing her response. This kiss was pure demand and she was helpless to refuse that demand, even if she'd wanted to. Her mouth opened to him, her tongue coming up to tangle with his.

Without quite knowing how it happened, Mitch found himself pushing Jenny back on the blanket, covering her body with his, deepening the kiss. Tasting her response only made him want more. He didn't think he could ever get enough of her.

His hands dragged impatiently at the soft T-shirt she wore, pulling it up to bare her midriff. Jenny felt his hand on her flat stomach, burning with a heat that had nothing to do with the warm summer night. And then it was moving upward. She held her breath and then her body went completely still as his fingers closed over her breast.

She felt the groan that rumbled in Mitch's chest when he found she wasn't wearing a bra, and she echoed it with a soft whimper of surprised pleasure. He swallowed the sound, making it his, just as she was his, she thought feverishly.

He caught her nipple between his thumb and forefinger and tugged gently, feeling the small nub harden beneath his touch. Her skin was as soft as rose petals. And her response was as hot as fire.

He shifted his attention to her other breast, teasing the same response from it, feeling her shiver with pleasure. Jenny arched her back instinctively, her fingers digging into his upper arms at the sensations he was sending through her.

Needing to see the response he could feel, Mitch dragged his mouth from hers, lifting his head to look down at her. Moonlight dusted her skin with silver-gold light, making her look something more than human. She dragged her eyelids open to look at him, her eyes deep, shadowy pools. He pulled his gaze from her face to look at the soft territory his hand had already claimed. Her breasts were high and firm, the nipples dusky shadows against the pale skin.

He had to taste her. Just once, he argued with the rapidly fading voice of his conscience. He'd stop this insanity then but not before he'd tasted the softness he'd uncovered.

He bent his head over her, his tongue coming out to flick across her swollen nipple. Jenny gasped, her whole body going rigid beneath him and then he opened his mouth over her and she melted.

It was as if the fireworks she'd been watching were inside her, showering sparks of sensation over her body. She'd never imagined it was possible to feel such an incredibly exquisite sensation. The feel of his mouth on her breast, his tongue laving her skin was so intense it was nearly a pain. Almost frightened, she buried her fingers in Mitch's thick dark hair, hovering uncertainly between pushing him away and drawing him closer.

And then he flexed his cheeks, sucking strongly on her nipple and her breath left her on a sob. Without conscious volition, her back arched, offering herself to him, her blood pounding with need.

Mitch felt her complete surrender. If he chose to take her right here and now, she wouldn't offer so much as a whisper of protest. He could ease the burning ache of hunger in both of them.

His mouth still at her breasts, his hand trailed across her flat stomach to find the waistband of her jeans. The button yielded easily and the zipper slid down with a whisper of sound. He laid his hand against her mound, sliding his fingers between her thighs. He could feel the damp heat of her through the fabric of her panties. She shivered as he stroked her, her hips moving into his touch.

He took his mouth from her breast to her mouth, catching the soft whimpering sounds she was making in the back of her throat. His tongue stabbed into her mouth even as his fingers found their way under the fragile shield of her underwear, easing into her heat.

He wanted her. Oh how he wanted her. It would be so easy to strip her clothes off, to spread her out on the blanket and sate himself with her. She burned for him, as hungry as he was. He could ease the ache in both of them. He arched his hips, pressing his rigid length against her thigh, torturing himself with the knowledge of how close fulfillment lay.

But the tiny thread that was all that remained of his conscience wouldn't let him take what she was so sweetly offering. No matter how right this felt, it was wrong. *He* was wrong.

He lifted his head to look down at her, seeing the flush of sexual desire that mantled her face, hearing her soft gasps of pleasure as he teased her closer to the peak. He couldn't have her, but he could give her this much.

Jenny felt Mitch's touch pushing her closer to some goal she could only imagine. Her whole body felt flushed and feverish, her skin burning hot. She shifted restlessly on the blanket and her hand came up to grasp his arm, half-wanting him to stop what he was doing. She couldn't bear it another moment. But she only clung to him, a deep feminine instinct telling her that the ease she sought lay at the end of the road he was pushing her along.

She could feel his eyes on her, watching her, witnessing her helpless response. There was something wildly erotic in having him watch her while his fingers worked such incredible magic. And then his thumb found the secret heart of her and she gasped, her back arching in shocked pleasure.

"Mitch!" His name was a thin cry, holding an edge of fear.

"Shh." He bent over her, his free hand locking in her hair, stilling the restless movements of her head. "Let go, sweetheart. I've got you safe."

And then he was giving her no choice. His mouth captured her keening cry as she tumbled over the edge into shuddering fulfillment.

Mitch held her, stroking her hair and soothing her with gentle kisses. Jenny's skin felt achingly sensitive and he seemed to understand that, keeping his touch soft, easing her back down.

She could never face him again. That was the first coherent thought she had. Never in a million years could she face him. Not after what had just happened. While her body felt heavy with sexual satisfaction, her mind was awash with embarrassment.

"Are you ever going to open your eyes again," he asked at last, his husky voice rich with soft amusement.

"No." But it hadn't sounded as if he thought she'd done something terrible, and she risked opening her eyes a little.

Mitch was looking down at her, his expression tender in the moonlight. Jenny felt her color come up and she turned her face away, hiding it against the arm he had braced next to her head.

"What's the matter?" he asked. He slid his fingers into her hair, using the hold to tug her gently out of hiding.

"You must think I'm dreadful," she whispered, staring at his collarbone.

"I think you're magnificent." He feathered a kiss along her cheekbone.

"You don't think it's terrible that we...that I..." She trailed off, unable to find the right words.

"I don't think you're terrible." He kissed her mouth, lingering until she kissed him back.

Her embarrassment faded, to be replaced by a delicious lethargy. She felt as if she could simply lie on this mountaintop forever with Mitch. The air was starting to cool as the day's heat dissipated in the thin mountain air, but she was warmed by an inner glow. She murmured a protest as he began tugging her T-shirt down.

"You're going to get chilled," Mitch said, his voice husky.

"I don't think I'll ever feel cold again." She caught his hand and brought it to her mouth, looking at him from under her lashes as she bit gently on the fleshy mound at the base of his thumb.

Mitch swallowed a groan and dragged his hand away. "You keep doing that and we're both going to go up in flames." His smile held a pained edge.

"Aren't you...I mean, aren't we going to..." She stopped, her cheeks flushing.

"I'm not and we're not." He eased her T-shirt over her breasts, his expression regretful.

"Don't you want me?" Jenny asked, her eyes showing hurt and confusion.

He took hold of her hand and dragged it down, pressing her palm against the front of his jeans. Her eyes widened and her breath caught as she felt the rigid length of him beneath the denim.

"Oh."

"Yeah, oh. I want you so bad, I'm probably going to suffer permanent damage," he said ruefully. He eased her hand away.

"Then why?"

"Because I've no intention of tumbling you on the ground like you were a peasant wench in a some old novel."

"We could go back to your place." Her cheeks felt as if they were on fire, but her eyes were steady on his.

If somebody was testing him, they were really determined to push the limits, Mitch thought, trying not to notice that her mouth was still swollen from his kisses.

"No." Exercising more willpower than he'd known he possessed, he sat up, dragging her with him. "I should be horsewhipped, as it is."

"Why? I'm not a child, Mitch." She frowned at him, feeling annoyance take the place of the delicious lethargy. She reached up to comb her hair back from her face and saw his eyes drop to where her breasts thrust against the front of her shirt. "You want me. You've admitted as much."

"I want a lot of things I can't have."

"But—"

"Don't." He put his hand over her mouth, his expression pained. "Don't tell me that I can have you, Jenny. Because I can't. It just isn't possible."

She tugged his hand away from her mouth. "Don't I get any say about it?"

"No." He softened the refusal with a smile. "I don't want to see you hurt, Jenny. I won't try to pretend I don't want you. I want you a hell of a lot, but in a couple of months, you're going off to college and I'll be leaving for good not long after. You're not built for a summer fling, Jenny. You'd end up badly burned and I'd end up with regrets. I don't want that for either of us."

Jenny lowered her eyes to hide the shimmer of tears. But there was a glint of determination behind her tears. The summer wasn't over yet.

Satisfied that she understood, Mitch stood up and drew her to her feet. Putting his arms around her, he brushed a kiss across her forehead.

The fireworks were over. It was time to take her home. But he made no move to release her. For a few minutes, he just wanted to hold her and pretend that he didn't ever have to let her go.

Chapter 6

She was in love.

Jenny had never been in love before, but she didn't need any experience to tell her how she felt now. She was in love with Mitch Sullivan. And it wasn't some kind of sexual infatuation caused by what had happened on the night of the Fourth.

Just thinking about what she'd let him do, about the uninhibited way she'd responded, was enough to make her face burn. But through the lingering embarrassment, she felt a new awareness of herself as a woman, of her own potential for pleasure.

It was the tenderness with which Mitch had treated her that made her realize her feelings. He'd been sensitive to what she was feeling, not just physically but emotionally. It would only have taken a word for her to have been reduced to total humiliation. Instead, he'd made her feel as if her response were natural and beautiful, nothing to be ashamed of. It was that concern for her feelings, that gentleness, that she'd fallen in love with.

She'd never in her life had anyone consider her feelings the way Mitch did. No one who'd ever thought that what was most important was what was best for her. She might disagree with him over what that was, but she could hardly fault him for putting her needs ahead of his own.

She loved him with the deep love of a woman, not the shallow love of a girl. She wanted this man to be part of her life forever. Jenny knew her own feelings. What she didn't know was just what he felt for her. Surely he must care for her a little; otherwise he wouldn't have treated her with such care.

Now she had two months to persuade him that he felt the same way about her that she did about him. Two months to convince him that the powerful attraction that lay between them was more than sexual. Two months before summer ended.

Mitch was in over his head and he knew it. He should have sent Jenny Monroe running the minute she showed up at the garage to thank him for coming to her rescue. He should have told her to take her flat tire somewhere else, even if it meant towing her car. Most of all, he should never have let himself be persuaded that a friendship was possible between them.

He couldn't even blame her for that. He'd known it wouldn't work, but he'd chosen to ignore his common sense. He'd pretended to himself that it *would* work because he'd wanted to keep on seeing her. He'd been a fool to give into that urge, and now he had to deal with the consequences. He had to convince Jenny to stay away from him.

But maybe not immediately, he thought, his hands on Jenny's slim waist, his mouth devouring hers.

All the resolutions in the world were of little use when he couldn't seem to keep his hands off Jenny. When she'd lifted her face, obviously expecting a kiss, Mitch had told himself it was a little silly not to kiss her, considering how intimate they'd been the night before.

But kissing Jenny Monroe was an addictive experience. Somehow, one kiss had led to another, until she'd broken away, flushed and breathless and looking so damned desirable he'd found himself regretting his nobility the night before. And then he could hardly tell her not to come around again after having just kissed her as if he thought tomorrow might not come.

So he didn't tell her that day. Or the next. And somehow, the day that followed didn't seem quite right. A week drifted by, and then another. Jenny came to the garage, but on several occasions, on his day off, Jenny would have the housekeeper make them a picnic and they'd go somewhere outside of town and spread a blanket on the thick green grass.

They ate and they talked. About his writing, about her classes. About whether or not space travel would become common in their lifetime. About whether or not Mrs. Callison was a kleptomaniac or just the most absentminded shopper in town.

And they kissed, though Mitch was careful to keep the situation under control, breaking it off before things went too far. Jenny didn't argue with him, accepting the limits he set without protest. The only problem was that he was taking so many cold showers he was starting to wonder whether or not he'd ever be able to father children again.

"Do you know what you're doing?"

Startled, Mitch turned to look at Jake, who'd come up behind him. Jake was watching Jenny's car as it pulled out of the parking lot. He pulled his gaze from the car and looked at his friend, his dark eyes concerned.

"No." Mitch's blunt answer drew a half smile that disappeared almost as soon as it came.

"She spends enough time here, she ought to be getting paid."

"It's summer. She's got a lot of time on her hands," Mitch said, wincing at the defensiveness he heard in his own voice.

"Well, time ain't what you've got on your hands. You've got trouble. Her daddy finds out she's spending so much time here and he's not going to be a happy camper about it."

"I doubt her father would notice if she was spending time with Charles Manson," Mitch said. He turned and walked back into the garage, picking up the tools he'd put down when Jenny arrived.

"Sooner or later, he'll notice this." Jake followed him and leaned one hip against the workbench. "Times may have changed, but there are still lines you don't cross. And the line between the Monroes and most of the rest of the world is one of those lines.''

"She's not royalty, for God's sake,'' Mitch snapped.

"In this town, she's close enough to it.'' Jake watched Mitch attack a rusted-on bolt, his expression worried. ''Ain't none of my business, man, but you could have chosen someone a little more accessible to fall in love with.''

"In love!'' Mitch dropped the wrench into the engine compartment as he whirled around to look at Jake. ''Who the hell said I was in love with her?''

"No one had to say anything. It's in your eyes when you look at her.''

"You're seeing things,'' Mitch snarled. ''Why don't you mind your own damned business. I can manage my life just fine without you giving me advice.''

"Sorry.'' Jake lifted his hands and shrugged an apology, recognizing that his friend was on the ragged edge of losing his temper. ''My mistake.''

Mitch spun back to the car without another word, listening as Jake moved off. He didn't immediately look for the wrench he'd dropped. He leaned his fists on the fender and stared at the engine in front of him.

Jake was nuts. He wasn't in love with Jenny Monroe. In lust. Maybe in like. But not in love. Only a fool would fall in love with someone he could never have. And he was many things, but a fool was not one of them.

At least it never had been before.

* * *

"Genevieve, I'd like to talk to you." Stephanie Monroe's tone held cool demand.

Jenny, on her way to her room, turned to look at her mother, her expression wary. Her mother rarely noticed her, unless it was to complain about something.

"It's late, Mother. Could it wait until morning?"

"It's not yet ten and I don't wish to wait until morning. Please come here."

The *please* was merely a polite convention, designed to make the order sound like a request. Jenny knew exactly what it was and she resented it. But there was no reason to refuse. As far as she knew, there was nothing in particular for her mother to be upset about. Maybe she actually wanted to say something pleasant, like "Congratulations on doing so well in your extra classes. I'm proud of you for getting such good grades."

Jenny rarely entered her mother's bedroom and, as always, the room struck her as being too perfect for comfort. Everything was done in shades of soft peach and ivory. It was like being in the midst of a confection, too feminine, too sweet, too everything.

Stephanie shut the door behind her daughter and crossed the ivory carpet to seat herself on a silk-covered boudoir chair. Crossing her long, slender legs at the ankle, she gestured to a matching fainting couch.

"Sit down, Genevieve."

"Sounds ominous," Jenny said lightly, trying to ignore the knot already forming in her stomach.

Stephanie didn't acknowledge her daughter's attempt at humor. Her jade-green eyes examined Jenny with a coolly impersonal expression that made Jenny want to check to see if her hair was combed. In her jeans and faded T-shirt, she felt woefully underdressed. But then she always felt that way around her mother. There was something intimidating about all that cool beauty.

Stephanie was wearing a pair of silk lounging pajamas exactly the color of her eyes. Her pale blond hair was cut short to frame her perfectly sculptured features. When Jenny was younger, she had thought that, if she were prettier, her mother might like her more. If only she'd inherited her mother's exquisite cheekbones and dark green eyes instead of her grandmother's rounded face and her father's more ordinary brown eyes, maybe Stephanie would have been able to love her.

She was old enough now to know that her mother's indifference would probably have become out-and-out dislike if her daughter had been beautiful enough to be perceived as competition. As it was, Jenny's main flaw was her mere existence, incontrovertible proof that Stephanie was no longer a young girl.

"Where were you tonight?"

"I was at Beth's. Why?"

"Beth?" Stephanie allowed a tiny frown to crease her smooth brow. "Oh, yes, that girl you went to school with."

It struck Jenny as ironic that she and Beth had been best friends for twelve years and her mother obviously couldn't even recall Beth's face.

"Who is this young thug you've been seeing?"

The question came without preamble. Jenny blinked, trying to shift her thinking. It hadn't occurred to her that her mother's sudden desire to talk to her had anything to do with Mitch.

"He's not a thug." The protest was the first thing that came to mind.

"That's not what I've been told."

"Well, you've been told wrong." Jenny struggled to match her mother's coolness and was rewarded by a flicker of surprise in Stephanie's eyes.

"I don't think so. Mitchell Sullivan has been arrested, more than once, I believe. He has a tendency to get involved in barroom brawls. His father was a drunk. His mother cleaned homes to support the two of them. The boy barely made it through school without getting expelled and he's done nothing with his life since except work as a mechanic in a low-level garage."

She reeled off the facts as if she were reading a police report. Jenny felt fear rise up in her throat, threatening to choke her. Despite Mitch's concern, she'd given no real thought to how her parents might react if they knew she was seeing him. She'd grown so accustomed to their lack of interest, it hadn't occurred to her that they'd care.

"If you know all that, then why did you ask me who he was?" She managed to maintain a calm façade, raising one brow in a cool imitation of her mother's expression. Annoyance flashed in the older woman's eyes, making her look almost human for a moment.

"Your attitude is inappropriate," she said in the same icy tone that had once struck absolute terror in her daughter's childish heart. But Jenny was older now and considerably less concerned with her mother's feelings.

"Perhaps you should tell me why you wanted to talk to me, Mother."

"Very well." Stephanie had herself back under control and Jenny knew she wouldn't be easily thrown off balance again. "You will stop seeing this ... man. Immediately."

"No." She'd had a chance to see where the conversation was going and her answer came without hesitation. "I'm no longer a child, Mother. You can't choose my friends for me anymore."

"I will not have you embarrassing the family by continuing this acquaintance."

"I don't see why my relationship with Mitch should be an embarrassment to the family."

"The man is obviously completely unsuitable." A flick of her hand dismissed Mitch as less than dirt, and Jenny felt her temper starting to slip.

"By whose standards?" she asked tightly. "Yours? I don't much care whether or not you think he's suitable."

"Have you slept with him?" The quick change of subject threw Jenny off balance and she answered without thinking.

"No! Not that it's any of your business," she added quickly, wishing that she'd thought to say that first.

"Well, at least you've shown some sense. You're not to see him again, not even to say goodbye."

"You're not listening to me," Jenny said, frustration making her voice shake. "I'm not going to stop seeing Mitch just because you say so. You can't make me." She regretted the childish challenge as soon as it was out.

"Don't be a fool, Genevieve. He's completely unsuitable. He's a mechanic, for God's sake. I'd have thought a daughter of mine would have better taste," she added, her eyes contemptuous as they flicked over the girl.

If Jenny had thought herself immune to her mother's dislike after all these years, she was discovering how wrong she'd been. That cold look cut like the flick of a whip, opening emotional wounds that had never really healed.

"I won't stop seeing him," she repeated stubbornly, incapable of any other response.

"I suppose you think you're in love with him," Stephanie remarked with disgust.

"My feelings have never concerned you before. I don't see any reason why they should now."

Jenny wanted to get up and leave. She didn't want to hear anything else her mother had to say. She just wanted to get out of this pastel prison and find Mitch. She wanted to feel his arms around her and hear him tell her everything was going to be alright.

"If you love him, you'll stop seeing him." Stephanie ignored Jenny's comment. "If you don't stop seeing him, I'll see to it that he's destroyed. Considering his reputation, it wouldn't take much. A few words in the right ears and he could be arrested for, oh, armed robbery perhaps. Who would believe he was innocent?''

Jenny stared at her, feeling physically ill. She'd long since come to terms with what her mother was, but she saw now that she'd never realized the full depth of her selfishness. Or just how far she'd go to get what she wanted.

"Don't look at me like that, Genevieve," Stephanie said impatiently. "I'm doing this for your good, as well as the family's. Eventually, you'll realize that I've saved you a great deal of heartache.

"From what I've been told of this man, he's had more than his fair share of experience with women. Just how long do you think you'd hold his interest anyway? I don't mean to be cruel, but you're hardly a beauty and, unless you've been leading a more interesting life than I think, you don't have the experience to keep him entertained with sex. At least this way, *you'll* be the one breaking it off and that will salve your pride a bit.''

For a moment, Jenny thought she might throw up. And wouldn't that make a mess of her mother's pristine carpet, she thought, feeling hysteria threaten.

She stood up and left the room without a word. Stephanie didn't try to stop her, no doubt assuming that she'd accomplished her goal. Though she'd managed to walk calmly from her mother's room, the moment the door shut behind her, Jenny ran as if the hounds of hell were on her heels. Taking the stairs at a breakneck pace, she snatched her purse off the hall table on her way out the door and ran for her car.

All she could think of was that she had to see Mitch. Though she'd never been to his home, she knew where he lived. He rented a place on the edge of town. The building had once been a storage shed and someone had converted it to what could be called a studio apartment, if you didn't mind being accused of exaggeration.

It had been raining all day, light showers that had turned to a downpour by midafternoon. Jenny wouldn't have noticed if it was snowing. She drove on automatic pilot, her one thought that Mitch could make things right again.

The drive that led up to Mitch's house was flooded, forcing her to park her car at its base and walk the rest of the way. Since she had neither coat nor umbrella, she was soaking wet by the time she arrived on the sagging porch. Lifting her hand, she rapped on the door.

Mitch had been sprawled on the bed, which offered the only seating in the small apartment. When he heard the knock, he muttered a curse, thinking it was probably Old Man Peterson coming to ask him to help tow his truck out of the mud. If the old man weren't too cheap to have his driveway graded, his truck wouldn't sink axle deep in mud every time it rained. He debated answering the door, but the light must be obvious and Peterson *was* his landlord.

He put down the book he'd been reading and went to the door, his feet silent on the cracked linoleum. Pulling open the door, he braced himself for an onslaught of Peterson's complaints about the weather. But it wasn't Peterson's lanky figure on the porch.

"Jenny! What are you doing here? For God's sake, you're soaked. Get in here." He reached out and drew her inside, shutting the door behind her.

"I had to come."

"What's wrong?" Mitch stepped in front of her, feeling something clench in his chest when he saw the look in her eyes. She looked devastated, her eyes a muddy brown from pain. "What's wrong, Jenny?"

"I had to come." She couldn't seem to say anything else.

Despite the rain, it was not particularly cold, but she was shivering convulsively. Though he suspected her chill was an inner one, getting her out of her wet clothes seemed like a reasonable first step toward getting her calmed down enough to tell him what had happened.

"You need to get out of those wet clothes. I'll get you a robe."

She watched as he went to the closet and pulled out a soft terry-cloth robe.

"I'm dripping all over your floor," she said when he returned.

"It would take more than water to hurt this floor. I doubt if battery acid would leave much impression on this stuff."

She nodded, oblivious to his attempt at humor. He started to tell her that she could change in the bathroom, but before he could speak, she looked up at him, her eyes brimming over with tears.

"Oh, Mitch. It was so awful."

Reacting instinctively, he reached out to put his arms around her. She seemed to crumple against him, as if his touch dissolved the last fragile threads of her control. He drew her into his arms, ignoring her incoherent protest that she'd get him wet.

"I dry," he said shortly. "Tell me what happened, Jenny."

But she seemed incapable of giving a coherent explanation. All he could gather was that she'd quarreled with her mother. And that it had been about him. The details weren't clear but maybe they weren't important. Obviously, whatever Stephanie Monroe had said, the words had cut deep. Mitch found himself wishing it weren't against his principles to hit a woman.

"I'm sorry," Jenny muttered at last, wiping her eyes with the handful of tissues he'd given her. "I'm sorry." The apology broke in the middle as a half sob shook her.

Mitch stroked her hair back from her forehead, his heart twisting as he looked down at her. He'd give his life to spare her pain, and yet all he could offer was a shoulder and some tissues.

"It's all right, sweetheart," he murmured, and Jenny felt the pieces of her world settle back into place. She wanted to believe him when he said that it was all right. She *needed* to believe him, at least for a little while.

"Oh, Mitch. Hold me."

"I will. As long as you want." He brushed a kiss on her forehead, across her damp eyelids. He tasted the salt tang of her tears and ached for her hurt. Wanting only to soothe her pain, his mouth settled on hers. The kiss was feather light, asking nothing, offering comfort.

Jenny's fingers curled into the fabric of his shirt, her head tilting back in an unconscious invitation to deepen the kiss. It seemed so natural that Mitch opened his mouth over hers without thinking, his tongue slipping between her lips to taste the sweet warmth of her mouth.

Afterward he could never pinpoint the moment when comfort flared into passion, when hunger edged out solace. The desire that was never far beneath the surface between them flashed suddenly white-hot. When he regained some of his senses, it was to find that they were lying on the bed, his body pressing Jenny into the mattress.

He stared down at her, trying to remember just how they'd gotten to this point. This wasn't what he'd intended. And he had to end it now before it got completely out of hand. But when he started to lift himself away from her, she caught hold of his shirt.

"Don't go. Make love to me. Please, Mitch, make love to me."

"Jenny..." He groaned a protest, trying not to notice the way her nipples pressed against the damp fabric of her T-shirt. "I can't."

"I want you." She *needed* him to. Maybe then, she'd be able to forget her mother's cruel words. She needed to prove to herself—to him—that he wanted her too much to resist.

"I want you, too, baby. But I can't. You're so young. You don't know what you're asking." She felt him tense and knew that once he left the bed, she'd have lost the battle.

"I'm not a virgin," she lied desperately. She felt him stiffen, but she couldn't bring herself to look at his face. Instead, she stared at the pulse that beat visibly at the base of his throat. "Brad and I were sleeping together before . . . before he got crazy."

Her words hit him like a blow to the solar plexus. He wanted to go find Brad Louderman and beat him to a pulp for daring to touch her. He wanted to tear him into small pieces and grind the pieces into the dirt.

At the same time, there was a certain shameful relief. She'd already slept with Louderman. It wasn't as if she were a complete innocent. Would it be so terrible if he took what she was offering? What he so desperately wanted?

"Jenny—"

"All that matters is that you want me." She slid her hands across his chest, bare between the open edges of his shirt. "And I want you." Later she'd wonder at her own boldness in practically begging him to make love to her. But she knew this was what was right. This was what had to happen.

"God knows I want you," Mitch said slowly, and she knew she'd won.

She buried her fingers in his hair as he lowered his head to hers, taking her mouth in a slow, drugging kiss that left her breathless and aching for more.

Outside, the rain pounded down. Lightning flashed over the mountains, followed by the deep roar of thunder. Inside, neither Mitch nor Jenny was aware of the storm outside—only the one inside.

Jenny's damp clothes seemed to melt away. The intensity of Mitch's gaze warmed her as quickly as if she were lying in front of a blazing fire. Any self-consciousness she might have felt burned away beneath the hunger in his eyes.

He stripped his shirt off his shoulders, tossing it heedlessly behind him. Holding Jenny's eyes with his, he lowered his torso slowly until the crisp hair on his chest just brushed against her puckered nipples. The sensation was exquisite torture.

If she thought she'd learned a great deal the night of the fireworks, she soon discovered her mistake. Mitch's hands played her slender body with all the skill of a virtuoso playing a violin. Effortlessly he stroked her to trembling arousal, whispering shockingly erotic promises in her ear.

When he stripped off his jeans and she got her first glimpse of a naked, aroused man, Jenny felt a surge of unease. Not for what was to come, but for the lie she'd told. But she wanted him too much to risk telling him the truth.

"Are you protected?"

Drowning in sensation, the husky question made no sense to Jenny at first. Protected from what? Dazed, she stared up at him. His meaning hit her at last. He was asking if she was likely to get pregnant. Pregnant with his child.

The thought brought a deep, visceral response. Mitch's child. If she was going to lose him, she might at least have that much. And deep down, she knew she was going to lose him. Her mother would find a way to drive them apart. But her mother wouldn't be able to do anything about a baby. And if there was a baby, maybe her mother wouldn't be able to drive Mitch away.

"Yes." The lie was out before she had a chance to change her mind.

"Good."

Mitch rose above her, his hips wedging her thighs apart. Jenny clung to his arms, her hands damp, her eyes suddenly full of uncertainty. She felt him against her, hard and smooth against her softness. She stared up into his face, seeing his features tighten as he eased into her.

"You're so tight. You feel wonderful."

She knew the exact moment he realized that she'd lied. His eyes flew open and he stared down at her in shock.

"Dammit, Jenny. You are a virgin." The husky words were almost an accusation.

"Don't go, Mitch. Please. This is what I want."

"God, I'm a man, not a saint," he told her on a groan.

He moved again, testing the strength of the barrier, watching her face for any sign of discomfort. But Jenny was too aroused to feel anything but impatience to know his full possession. She arched her hips in silent demand. Groaning, Mitch lowered his body to covers hers. He slid his hands beneath her and hooked them over her shoulders.

"Hang on to me, sweetheart. I want you with me every step of the way."

His mouth swallowed her gasp of pain as he sheathed himself in her. But the discomfort was only momentary and he soon taught that the pleasure that came after was nearly endless. He rocked against her, gently at first, allowing her time to adjust to his invasion of her body.

Within seconds, Jenny had forgotten the pain. There wasn't room for anything but the spiraling pleasure that licked out to consume every inch of her body. She arched against him, her hands sliding restlessly up and down his back as the pleasure spun higher, pushing her upward.

This time, she thought she knew what awaited her. But nothing had prepared her for the intensity of sharing her body with the man she loved. She felt the shivering sensation begin deep inside and threw her head back against the pillow, her neck arched as wave after wave of pleasure washed over her.

Mitch felt the delicate inner contractions grip him and he looked down at Jenny, watching the flush that ran up over her breasts before flooding her features. The sight was enough to send him spinning headlong after her.

Feeling him shudder in her arms, Jenny found her own pleasure heightened by the knowledge that she'd given him this. Whatever the future held for them, she'd have this moment to hold close forever. Sliding her arms around his sweat-dampened back, she drew him down, cradling him as the shock waves of fulfillment gripped his big frame.

It was a long time later before either of them spoke. Jenny lay cradled against Mitch's side, her body so close to his that not even a shadow could have slipped between them.

"You lied to me about sleeping with Louderman."

"Yes." She didn't apologize. She felt no regret for the lie and she didn't pretend otherwise.

"I could have hurt you."

"You didn't." Her eyes were on the lazy movement of her fingers as they combed through the mat of black hair on his chest.

Outside, the storm sounded as if it were starting to fade, the rain still falling but without the sound and fury it had displayed earlier. She wanted to call the storm clouds back. For some reason, it seemed as if as long as the storm lasted, nothing could threaten the contentment she'd found.

"What else did you lie to me about, Jenny?"

Her fingers stilled and she closed her eyes. It sounded as if he already knew the answer to that question, and she wasn't at all sure he was going to be as forgiving of the second lie as he had the first.

"You're not on the pill, are you?" he asked, reading the answer in her silence.

"No," she whispered. "But it's not a bad time of month for me," she added quickly, tilting her head to look up at him.

"Do you have any idea how many kids are around today because it 'wasn't a bad time of the month'?" His eyes held a mixture of anger and despair.

"I'm sorry. I didn't want you to stop."

"I couldn't have stopped if someone had pointed a gun at my head. But I could have used a condom. That was why I asked if you were protected."

"I'm sorry," she said again.

"No. I'm the one who's sorry." He reached up to run his fingers through her tangled hair and she saw that his anger was self-directed. "I think I knew you were lying about Louderman, but I wanted to believe you. I wanted to have an excuse to do what I've been aching to do ever since I met you. I should have been thinking more clearly."

"I shouldn't have lied about it, Mitch. That was stupid and...childish of me."

He knew what that admission must have cost her and his expression softened. He cupped her chin in his hand, studying her face with dark blue eyes.

"If you're pregnant, I'll take care of you, Jenny. We'll work everything out. I'll see that you don't suffer for my impatience."

"Oh, Mitch." Tears burned in her eyes and she blinked to dispel them. The words simply couldn't be held back another minute.

"I love you, Mitch."

His hand tightened on her chin as she saw some emotion flicker across his face, but it was gone so quickly she couldn't be sure of what it was. Despair?

The silence stretched as his eyes searched her face. Just when she was sure he was going to let her declaration go unanswered, the arm that lay across her back tightened, drawing her even closer.

"I love you, too, Jenny. God help us both, but I love you, too."

Chapter 7

They slept, woke to make love again and slept again. There was no talk of the future. For the moment, wrapped in the newness of their love, anything seemed possible, even a future together.

Her mother's threats seemed much less frightening with Mitch holding her close. His arms felt so strong and sure around her, Jenny couldn't believe there was anything Stephanie could do to separate them.

The storm faded away completely sometime in the hours after midnight, and, snuggled close to Mitch, Jenny fell asleep, convinced that everything was going to be all right.

Mitch didn't completely share her optimism, but he did feel a contentment he'd never known before. Despite everything that told him it was wrong, Jenny felt so right in his arms he found himself wondering if things couldn't work out after all.

She loved him. That had to count for something. He'd never had anyone tell him they loved him, and he'd never realized how that simple statement could shift a man's whole perspective.

She was young, he cautioned himself. At eighteen, he'd been older than she was now, but life had forced him to grow up quickly. For all the emptiness in her family, Jenny had still been sheltered. She couldn't possibly understand just how cold the real world could be. And if she announced that she was in love with him, there was the possibility that her parents would disown her. How long would her love last if she was faced with real hardship?

God knows what they'd do if she turned out to be pregnant. But they'd cross that bridge, if and when they came to it. In the morning, he'd get a clearer explanation of her quarrel with her mother. Then they'd have to decide where to go from here. Just pray she wasn't pregnant.

Closing his eyes, he drifted to sleep, unaware that his hand was pressed possessively over her flat stomach.

The sound of someone banging on the front door brought Mitch awake with a suddenness that had his heart pounding in his chest. The room was pitch-black, adding to his initial feeling of disorientation.

"What is it?" Jenny's voice was frightened, responding to the panic that always comes with any summons in the middle of the night.

"It's nothing." Mitch reassured her automatically, though he had no idea whether or not it was the truth.

Fumbling in the dark, he groped for the alarm clock and the lamp at the same time.

When the light came on, he was momentarily blinded by it and had to wait for his eyes to adjust. Four o'clock. No one knocked on a door at four in the morning unless it was an emergency.

He swung his legs off the bed. His jeans were on the other side of the room and whoever it was had started knocking again. Cursing, he dragged the bedspread off the foot of the bed and wrapped it around his hips as he stumbled to the door. A glance over his shoulder showed him that Jenny was sitting up in bed, the covers pulled over her breasts, her hair a tangled cloud on her shoulders and her eyes wide and frightened.

Mitch pulled open the door, careful to stand in front of the opening so that Jenny would not be seen.

"Jake! What the hell are you doing here?"

"I saw Jenny's car at the bottom of the drive," Jake said, ignoring the question. "Is she here with you?"

"Why?"

"There's been an accident. Her dad's been taken to the hospital," Jake said, pitching his voice so that it wouldn't carry beyond the two of them. "Billy and I were heading up the canyon to fish," he said, mentioning his older brother, "and we heard the report. When we drove by your place and saw the car, I figured she might not know."

"Jesus." The word was more prayer than curse. Mitch thrust his fingers through his hair, oblivious to the chill predawn air on his bare chest. "Thanks, man. I owe you one."

"Tell Jenny I hope her dad's all right."

"Yeah. I will." Mitch shut the door and stood staring at it for a moment before turning to face Jenny. She obviously already knew something was wrong and there seemed no way to soften the news.

"There's been an accident," he said flatly. "Your father's in the hospital. Get dressed and I'll take you there."

Jenny was pale but calm as Mitch parked her car in the hospital parking lot. She hadn't said much since he'd given her the news. But then, what was there to say? Until they knew something more than just the bald fact that there'd been an accident, there wasn't much either of them could say.

Jenny's hand reached for his as they walked through the hospital doors. Mitch's fingers closed over hers, hard and strong, offering nonverbal reassurance.

The nurse at the desk directed them to the waiting room, saying only that Willard Monroe was still in surgery and she really couldn't tell them anything more than that. Feeling Jenny shudder at the mention of surgery, Mitch wrapped his arm around her shoulders and led her to the waiting room.

As they pushed open the door, Stephanie Monroe turned from the window. Jenny stopped just inside the room when she saw her mother. Mitch looked from one to the other, seeing the resemblance between them. It was there in the shape of the mouth, in the curve of the jaw. But as far as he was concerned, Stephanie's icy features fell far short of Jenny's gentle warmth.

"Mother. Is there any word about Daddy?"

Stephanie didn't answer immediately. Her jade-green eyes skimmed over her daughter, taking in the man's shirt that topped her jeans, covering her almost to the knee. From the lack of makeup and the hastily combed hair, it must have been obvious that she'd just climbed out of bed.

Stephanie's gaze shifted to Mitch, noting the protective arm around Jenny's shoulders and the cool hostility in the blue eyes. Mitch read her thoughts and knew it must be obvious to anyone who looked at them that they'd been in the same bed.

"Mother?" Jenny prompted her, her voice tight with fear.

"There's no word." Stephanie looked at her daughter, her eyes as cold as ice. "They don't know if he'll live."

Mitch felt the harsh announcement strike Jenny with the force of a blow and his arm tightened around her, trying to absorb some of the impact.

"What . . . what happened?" Jenny had to struggle to keep her voice steady.

"He was worried about you when you didn't come home. He went out looking for you and apparently lost control of the car and skidded into a tree. He was probably too worried to be paying close attention to the road," she added, in case the knife hadn't been sunk deep enough already.

"That's enough." Mitch actually shifted his position so that he stood between the two women.

"I think my daughter should know exactly what the results of her promiscuity may be, Mr. Sullivan. I assume you're Sullivan," she inquired, as if Jenny slept with so many men she couldn't keep them all straight.

"I'm Mitch Sullivan. And Jenny has nothing to feel guilty about, no matter what happens with her father."

"Perhaps you're right." Stephanie's tone left room for considerable doubt. "Would you mind leaving us alone, Mr. Sullivan. I think this is a time when only the family should be here."

"I'm staying with Jenny," he said flatly, determined to offer her what support he could.

"Maybe it would be best if you left, Mitch." Jenny's voice was thin but steady.

Mitch turned to look at her, his heart twisting at the sight of her pinched white face. Her eyes were so dark they were almost black and they seemed to have a hard time focusing on him.

"I can stay," he said, not wanting to leave her alone with her mother.

"No, really, I think it would be best if you left." She gestured vaguely in her mother's direction, seeming to indicate that his presence was adding to the tension.

And perhaps it was, he admitted reluctantly. Certainly Stephanie Monroe wanted him gone, and she was obviously a woman accustomed to getting her own way.

"Are you sure?" he asked, taking Jenny's hands in his. They were like ice and he cupped them between his, trying to give her some of his warmth.

"Yes. I'll let you know how my father is." She gave him a vague smile and pulled her hands away to clasp them in front of her.

"Call if you need me," he said, moving reluctantly toward the door.

"I doubt your services will be needed, Mr. Sullivan," Stephanie said coolly. Mitch ignored her, his worried eyes searching Jenny's face.

"You'll call if you need me." He made the words half an order, half a question, and she nodded.

"Of course."

Unsatisfied with her answer but seeing no choice, Mitch left, feeling as if he were abandoning her just when she needed him most.

Standing in the brightly lit hallway, he thrust his fingers through his hair, wondering how it was possible for everything to change so completely in the space of less than an hour.

Pushing his way outside, he saw that dawn was starting to break, casting pale pink fingers across the gray sky. He'd always thought of dawn as a hopeful time, but he didn't feel particularly hopeful at the moment. No matter how much he wanted to believe otherwise, he had the feeling that, live or die, Willard Monroe's accident had put an insurmountable wall between him and Jenny.

Mitch didn't hear from Jenny, but it wasn't hard to find out how Willard Monroe was doing. In fact, it would have been difficult to *avoid* hearing about his progress. With the Monroe Furniture Works the town's largest employer, Ransome held its collective breath, waiting to see what would happen.

So Mitch knew that he survived the surgery and that the doctors were cautiously optimistic. He also knew when it was discovered that Monroe was expected to live but that the accident had left him paralyzed from the waist down.

Almost any conversation in the town, sooner or later, turned to a discussion of what Monroe's paralysis might mean. Would he be able to keep up with his work? Would he sell the plant and would a new owner want to make a lot of changes? Speculation ran rampant, new rumors feeding on the old since there was a dearth of fact.

When Jenny didn't call in the first couple of days, Mitch called the Monroe house, only to be told that Miss Monroe was at the hospital with her father. Unwilling to go to the hospital and risk running into Stephanie, which could only cause trouble, Mitch waited another forty-eight hours and then tried again. This time, Miss Monroe was "unavailable to take his call."

He hung up the phone and stared at it for a long time, debating his next move. Did he just wait for her to contact him? Or did he go up to that big house and demand to see her?

Why hadn't she called?

Jenny hadn't called, because she didn't think she could bear to see Mitch without breaking down. She was only hanging on to her self-control by the skin of her teeth, as it was. If she saw Mitch, he'd want to help her and there was nothing he could do for her now. Nothing anyone could do to ease the guilt that ate into her like acid.

Her father's accident was her fault. That fact had been hard enough to bear when she'd been able to tell herself that he was going to be all right. But when the doctors gave them the news about his paralysis, the guilt became a nearly crippling burden, one she deserved.

If it hadn't been for her, he wouldn't have been out driving in the rainstorm and he wouldn't have been distracted enough to lose control of the car.

And it only made it worse that he didn't seem to blame her. When they finally allowed her in to visit him, he didn't utter a single word of reproach but only smiled at her and held out his hand.

Jenny was too burdened with guilt to find the words to tell him how terrible she felt about being the cause of his accident. She could only sob brokenly and tell him she loved him. And he stroked her hair and told her he loved her, too.

At night, she tossed and turned, her thoughts as restless as her body. Guilt made an uneasy company for her insomnia. Guilt over her father's accident. Guilt over the lies she'd told Mitch. Somehow, in her sleep-starved, overwrought mind, the two became entangled, as if the lies had led to her father's accident.

Mitch had said from the start that it wouldn't work, she remembered, staring up at the dark ceiling. But she hadn't listened. She'd been so sure that she knew better. So damned sure. And look where it had all led. If she hadn't pursued Mitch, her father would never have wrecked his car.

In her fevered state, the logic seemed obvious, as did the solution. It was her involvement with Mitch that had caused this terrible thing to happen. Ending that involvement was the only possible course of action.

The decision sent a stabbing pain through her heart, which was no more than she deserved, she thought. She didn't deserve to be happy, not after what she'd done. If she tried for the rest of her life, it still wouldn't be possible to make up to her father for the damage she'd done.

She'd go to Mitch and tell him that she didn't want to see him again. He'd probably be relieved. No doubt he'd only said he loved her because he felt guilty about sleeping with her. Rolling over, she buried her face in her pillow and sobbed as if her heart were breaking, which is exactly what it was doing.

"Jenny's here, Mitch."

Mitch had been attempting to seat a particularly stubborn manifold cover into place, but at Jake's announcement he jerked his head out of the engine compartment, looking over his shoulder at his friend.

"Take care of this, would you?"

Jake nodded and reached in to take the manifold out of his hands. "She's in the office," he said.

"Thanks." Mitch grabbed a rag off the bench and wiped his hands as he strode toward the office.

Two weeks since her father's accident. Two weeks since they'd made love. The longest two weeks he'd ever spent in his life. He'd already made up his mind to track her down tonight after work, whether at the hospital or at home. Stephanie Monroe be damned, he had to see Jenny. And now, here she was.

Jenny spun to face him as he pushed open the office door. If Mitch had expected her to run into his arms, he was doomed to disappointment. She stood in front of the big desk, staring at him with wide eyes, looking as if she were more likely to run *from* him than to him.

"Hi." Mitch shut the door behind him, noticing the way her eyes followed the movement, as if she wished he'd left it open. Mitch felt a knot start to coil in his stomach.

"Hi," she said, looking everywhere but at him.

"How are you?" He stayed by the door, sensing that the last thing she wanted was to have him come closer.

"I'm fine."

The conventional reassurance was obviously untrue. Just looking at her, Mitch could see that she was anything but fine. She'd lost weight and her too-pale skin was stretched taut over her cheekbones. She wore a black T-shirt that emphasized her pallor, and she'd scraped her hair back into a ponytail that revealed the new hollows in her cheeks.

"How's your father?"

"Paralyzed." The stark answer held a world of pain. Mitch curled his fingers into his palms, holding back the urge to go to her and take her in his arms. Everything about her said that the last thing she wanted was to be touched.

"I'm sorry," he said simply, wishing he could find the right words to ease her pain.

"So am I," she said wearily. And then the stiff mask cracked for a moment, allowing him a glimpse of pure anguish. "It's so terrible, Mitch. To see him lying there and know that he's never going to walk again."

He would have gone to her then and taken her in his arms, but she stiffened, the mask snapping back into place immediately. Mitch froze, feeling the walls come up around her.

He didn't offer her any of the clichés about people with handicaps leading full, productive lives. That wasn't what she needed right now. What she needed was to know that her father was going to walk again, and that was something he couldn't give her.

"I tried to get hold of you," he said at last, when the silence had stretched awkwardly.

"I know." She lifted one shoulder in a half shrug. "I just haven't been up to talking to anyone."

Anyone. Was that all he was? Just another person calling to offer sympathy? The knot in his stomach coiled tight and hard as he searched her face, looking for some sign that she remembered telling him she loved him. But there was nothing there to indicate that that night had ever happened.

"I can't see you again," she said abruptly. Her eyes skimmed across his face and then focused on the calendar pinned to the wall. "You were right, all those times you said it would never work out between us. I was just too stubborn to admit it."

"I thought it was working out pretty well," Mitch said slowly, trying to see past the rigid mask of her face.

"Well, it wasn't. You said I was too young and you were right. I've gotten a lot older in the last two weeks and I've had a chance to realize that you were right from the start.''

"Jenny, if you're feeling guilty because of your father's accident, it wasn't your fault.''

"I know that.'' Jenny forced a meaningless smile. She'd had plenty of time to anticipate what he might say. Naturally he'd feel obliged to protest her decision. For all his reputation as a hell-raiser, she knew Mitch was a man who took his responsibilities seriously. He'd feel obligated to argue with her decision, even if he was secretly relieved by it.

"This has nothing to do with my father's accident,'' she lied. "Although that's made me realize the truth sooner than I would have otherwise.''

"You sounded pretty sure of your feelings the other night,'' he said, and she had to conceal a wince at the reminder of that night.

"I read once that women have a tendency to confuse love with sex.''

"So that's all it was?'' Mitch asked. "Just sex?''

"That's all it was.''

She forced herself to meet his searching look, keeping her expression indifferent. For a moment, she almost thought she saw hurt in his eyes. But she knew that was her imagination. For him to be hurt, he'd have to really love her and that wasn't possible.

"Jenny—''

"I really don't want to talk about it, Mitch,'' she interrupted. "No sense in beating a dead horse.''

Jenny knew she had to get out of the office, had to get away from him before she did something stupid, like throw herself against him and beg him to tell her that he loved her. This was the price she had to pay for the tragedy she'd caused.

"I think we should talk," Mitch said.

"There's nothing to talk about." She moved toward the door and, after a moment's hesitation, Mitch moved aside.

"Are you sure this is what you want?" he asked as she took hold of the doorknob.

What she wanted? What she wanted was for everything to be the way it had been two weeks ago. What she wanted was for her father to walk again. For this burden of guilt to be lifted. But what she wanted and what was going to happen were two different things.

"It's what I want," she said without turning to look at him. Before she could change her mind, she pulled open the door and left.

Mitch watched her go, wondering if he should have stopped her. His every instinct told him that she'd been lying through her teeth. She was upset over her father's accident, and despite her denial, he knew she felt as if she were to blame for it. Maybe she felt that, by ending their relationship, she was somehow making up for what had happened to her father.

Or was it just that he wanted to believe that?

He rubbed one hand tiredly over his face, wishing there was some way for him to know the truth. What was real and what was just what he desperately wanted to believe?

The only thing he was sure of was that he wasn't going to let it end so easily. He'd give her a few more days and then he'd go and see her again.

* * *

Standing on the front porch of the Monroe home, Mitch had the uneasy feeling that he was making a big mistake. He'd been right from the start, he thought, turning to look out at the immaculate expanse of lawn. What could he possibly have in common with a girl who'd grown up in a house like this?

But they'd had something in common, his mind insisted stubbornly. They'd fallen in love. Maybe he was a fool, but he couldn't quite believe that that hadn't been real.

When the door opened, he turned, his shoulders stiffening imperceptibly when he saw Stephanie Monroe standing in the doorway. If she was surprised to see him, it didn't show.

"Mr. Sullivan. I had a feeling we'd be seeing more of you." Spoken by someone else, the words could have been congenial. Spoken by Stephanie, he was made to feel like a particularly annoying encyclopedia salesman.

"I'd like to see Jenny," he said, by way of greeting.

"I'm sure you would." Stephanie hesitated a moment before stepping back and holding the door open. "Perhaps you should come in, Mr. Sullivan. I think we should talk."

"I can't imagine what we would have to talk about, Mrs. Monroe." Mitch stepped into the marble-tiled foyer. "Is Jenny home?"

"As a matter of fact, she is home." If it had been anyone else, Mitch might have thought that she looked distressed, but he couldn't imagine this woman ever feeling anything less than in complete control. "Come into the study, please, Mr. Sullivan. Jenny asked me to speak to you."

"*Jenny* asked you to speak to me?" He followed her automatically, stepping into the book-lined study and turning as she closed the door behind them. "Why would Jenny ask you to speak to me?"

"Actually, she heard your arrival," Stephanie said. "Your motorcycle is rather loud." She gave him a quick smile to show that she meant no criticism, and Mitch was struck again by the elusive resemblance between mother and daughter. When she smiled like that, she reminded him of Jenny.

"Why don't you sit down?" She settled herself in a huge leather chair that dwarfed her slim figure, making her seem almost fragile in comparison.

"I'll stand, if you don't mind. You said Jenny heard me arrive."

"Yes. And she asked me to talk to you." Stephanie smoothed one slender finger along the crease of her pearl-gray trousers. "These past two weeks have been very difficult for her, for both of us, really. I think she just didn't feel quite up to facing you."

"Jenny's never had any trouble facing me before," Mitch said slowly.

"Things have changed. I know Jenny told you that she didn't wish to see you anymore," she told him.

If Mitch hadn't been thrown off balance by her words, he might have noticed the quick look she slanted him, gauging his reaction.

"She was upset," he said. "She feels guilty about her father's accident. Guilt you're responsible for."

"Yes, I know. Those terrible things I said at the hospital. Believe me, I'd give anything to take those words back." She shook her head, and when she lifted her eyes to his, they were shimmering with unshed tears. "I was so upset and frightened, I hardly knew what I was saying. But that didn't give me the right to strike out at Jenny."

"No, it didn't." But his tone wasn't as harsh as it might have been. He felt as if he were seeing two pictures, one laid on top of the other and he wasn't sure which one he should believe. Was she the icy woman who'd been so cruel or was she the penitent mother he saw now?

"When Jenny heard your arrival, she asked me if I'd see you. She asked me to tell you that she meant what she said earlier. She doesn't wish to see you again."

Odd, how the words sounded so much more believable coming from her mother than they had when Jenny had said them.

"I'd prefer to hear that from Jenny, herself, if you don't mind."

Stephanie sighed and stood up. "I thought you might feel that way. Jenny asked me to give you this." She reached into her pocket and pulled out the silver locket he'd given Jenny for her birthday. Dangling from her mother's manicured fingers, surrounded by the exquisitely decorated room, the inexpensive little trinket looked cheap.

Mitch reached out to take it from her automatically. Was it possible to actually feel an emotional blow, he wondered vaguely.

"She said to tell you that, while the gift meant a great deal to her, she doesn't feel right about keeping it now."

Mitch stared at the locket in silence before closing his fingers slowly over it. He lifted dull eyes to her face, seeing nothing but compassion there.

"Jenny's still very young, Mitch," she said gently. He wondered when he'd ceased to be "Mr. Sullivan" and become Mitch. Maybe when it became obvious that he wasn't a threat to her daughter anymore?

"I don't mean to be unkind, but you are quite a bit older than she is. Perhaps you should have realized that, at eighteen, love isn't quite as permanent as it is when one is older."

Wasn't that exactly what he'd thought? What he'd tried to tell Jenny? Wasn't this why he'd tried to keep his distance, to keep things from getting serious between them? Only he'd finally let himself believe that he was wrong. He opened his hand and dropped his gaze to it.

"She could be pregnant."

If he'd have been looking at her, he would have seen the quick anger that twisted Stephanie's features for just an instant. But when she spoke, her tone was even, still holding the underlying note of pity that grated at his pride.

"She told me that. She took the responsibility for it, said you weren't to blame."

Mitch said nothing. He wondered if she'd told her mother that she'd lied to him.

"What if she's pregnant?" he asked, looking at Stephanie.

"We discussed that. At Jenny's age, I don't think she should be forced to pay for a mistake for the rest of her life."

The delicate phrasing didn't conceal her meaning, and Mitch felt the final nail sink into the coffin holding his hopes. His very foolish hopes, he saw now.

"It seems you've thought of everything," he said at last.

"Jenny is my daughter and I love her very much. Naturally, I want to protect her as much as I can."

"Naturally." He pushed the necklace into his pocket.

"I know Jenny didn't mean to hurt you," Stephanie said gently. But her sympathy was like salt in a raw wound.

"Save it," he said shortly. "It's no big deal."

"I am sorry."

But Mitch was already on his way out, jerking open the study door and striding across the foyer to the front door. He felt as if he were suffocating in the big house. Straddling his bike, he cast one last look at its elegant facade.

Hell, he should have known better than to try to cross the tracks, he thought bitterly. Gunning the motor, he sent the bike down the driveway.

Inside, Stephanie Monroe shut the front door Mitch Sullivan hadn't bothered to close and turned away from it, her expression content.

"Was that Mitch?" Jenny ran down the stairs, her hair still wet from the shower, a heavy velour robe thrown hastily over her damp body.

"Yes, it was." Stephanie crossed the foyer to the study as if there were nothing more to be said.

"What did he want?" Jenny followed her mother, stopping in the doorway.

Stephanie flicked an imaginary piece of dust off the Staffordshire dog that sat on the hearth. She made an infinitesimal adjustment in the position of one of the flowers in the arrangement that filled the fireplace.

"Mother. What did he say?"

"The Sullivan boy?" Stephanie asked, as if they'd been talking about someone else. "He came to say goodbye. I told him you were in the shower but he refused to wait."

"Goodbye?" Jenny's fingers clenched around the doorjamb as she felt her knees weaken. She hadn't realized until just that moment how much she'd been counting on Mitch to see through her insistence that they not see each other—how much she'd hoped he'd want to see through it.

"Why was he saying goodbye? Is he going to Europe now? Is that where he's going?"

"He did say something about Europe," Stephanie said slowly, as if it hadn't been important enough to remember.

"I . . . didn't think he'd just leave," Jenny said, her eyes dazed.

"I don't know why you're so surprised, Genevieve. He said you'd told him that you didn't want to see him anymore."

"Yes." Since she hadn't said a word to her mother about her talk with Mitch, *he* must have been the one to tell her. "But I didn't think he'd just go."

"Well, he did. And it's just as well. He was a thoroughly impossible man for you, anyway. You'll get over your infatuation soon enough." With a flick of her fingers, she dismissed Jenny's feelings as too ephemeral to be of any real importance.

Her dark green eyes skimmed over her daughter. Jenny looked as if she'd been dealt a blow from which she wasn't sure she could recover. But there was no particular sympathy in Stephanie's eyes.

"I just didn't think he'd go," Jenny said again. Tears rose in her eyes, too quick for her to conceal. "I love him." A sob rose in her throat, choking her voice. "I love him."

"Stop it!" Her mother moved so quickly there was no time to avoid the quick slap that snapped Jenny's head to the side.

Shock dried her tears instantly. She'd never been struck by either of her parents, and she couldn't quite believe that her mother had really hit her. But there was no ignoring her burning cheek. She stared at her mother, her eyes wide and shocked.

"Don't start crying over that hoodlum," Stephanie snapped impatiently. "Don't ever forget that your father is paralyzed because of your infatuation with him. Do you want to risk killing him by chasing after a man who obviously doesn't want you anymore?"

Jenny pressed her hand to her hot cheek, feeling the burden of guilt sink like a thousand-pound weight onto her shoulders. Her mother was right, no matter what her motives—and Jenny didn't have much faith in those. But nothing could change the facts.

Her father's condition was her fault. He'd been looking for her, worried about her. And he'd never walk again because of that concern. She could never make that up to him. Not if she spent the rest of her life trying.

And now that Mitch was gone, she had nothing else to do with her life but try to make up to her father for the loss of his legs.

Chapter 8

Ten Years Later

Mitch slowed the Harley motorcycle to a stop at the light where Maple crossed Main and braced his booted feet on either side of the big bike. The town hadn't changed much, he thought. Oh, it had grown some. There was a new sprawl of gas stations and fast-food restaurants on the edge of town. And he'd seen a poster advertising a multiplex cinema on Harvard. Ten years ago, Ransome had boasted only two theaters, both built in the sixties and sporting screens of a size rarely seen these days.

Ransome had certainly changed some, but not as much as he'd expected. From the looks of things, it was still virtually a one-employer town. And that employer was Monroe Furniture Works. He'd made it a point to keep track of the company over the years, and he knew they'd done well in a time when many family-owned companies were either failing or being absorbed by large corporations.

Not that he had any real interest in the factory or the Monroe family. Or for that matter, in Ransome. He'd been gone for ten years, and the old home ties had been stretched so thin they had all but disintegrated. It was curiosity more than anything else that had brought him back. Curiosity and a faint tugging on those tattered ties.

Mitch gave the bike gas as the light changed, following a battered green pickup truck through the intersection, his eyes noting the changes along the street. He flicked on his turn signal. The corner was so familiar that it was possible to believe he'd gone back in time, that the past ten years had never happened.

But if the street hadn't changed, he had. He'd come a long way from the angry young man who'd left, a very long way.

He turned into the parking lot in front of Eddie's Garage and let the bike idle to a stop in front of one of the repair bays. Nudging the kickstand in place, he swung off the bike. Narrowing his eyes against the hot July sun, he looked at the building. Another place where the changes had been minimal. A new coat of paint maybe, but it had had time to weather to the same vague pinkish gray as the old coat.

"Can I help you?"

Mitch swung toward the voice, his mouth curving in a smile.

"Well, that all depends," he said. He saw Jake's eyes widen in recognition.

"Mitch! Mitch Sullivan, you dog! What are you doing back in Ransome?"

The two men shook hands, laughing their pleasure at seeing each other again after so many years.

"I was in the neighborhood and thought I might as well drop by and see if you'd been keeping yourself out of trouble."

"Always, man. You know me."

"Yeah. That's why I thought I ought to check up on you," Mitch said dryly.

"You were the hell-raiser, not me," Jake said, laughing. "I was the dull one, remember?"

"I seem to remember you raising a little hell of your own, a time or two."

"Maybe. But I'm a respectable married man, these days."

"Married!" Mitch's brows rose in exaggerated surprise. "Is this the man who said that marriage was nothing but a trap?"

"Yeah, well, even the best of us fall into that trap."

Since he looked more than content, Mitch suspected he'd walked into that particular trap with his eyes wide open and a smile on his face.

"So, who is she?"

It wasn't anyone Mitch had known, but Jake just happened to have pictures of her, as well as half a dozen photos of his three-year-old daughter. Mitch looked at them all and made appropriate comments. It seemed that things weren't quite as unchanged as they'd at first seemed. Not only was Jake a husband and a father, but he was now the owner of Eddie's Garage.

"Old Man Riker packed up and moved to Tahiti three years ago. Said he was getting too old to be spending winters where the snowdrifts were taller than he was. My dad helped me scrape up some money and I convinced the bank I was a good risk and I bought Riker out."

"You didn't change the name," Mitch commented, nodding to the sign painted across the front of the building.

"No." Jake followed his gaze. "I thought about it, but the place just wouldn't look right with any other name painted up there."

"I suppose not."

"So what are you doing?" Jake asked, turning back to Mitch. "I think the last I heard of you was a postcard from Spain. That was eight or nine years ago."

"Writers are notoriously poor correspondents," Mitch admitted, shrugging an apology.

"So your gamble paid off. I thought you were nuts when you quit and said you were off to Europe to try your hand at writing full-time."

"I've done well enough," Mitch said, not bothering to mention that his latest book was hovering on the bestseller lists. That was all part of another life—the life he'd built since leaving Ransome. At the moment, he didn't want that life to intrude on the old memories.

The talk shifted to people they'd known—who'd married whom, who'd gotten divorced, how many kids they'd all had. Listening to Jake talk, Mitch felt swept back in time. The same people were doing the same things, though in a lot of cases, they were doing it with new partners.

"What about Jenny Monroe?" Mitch was half surprised to hear himself asking the question. He'd thought that he had no more interest in Jenny than in half a dozen other people whose names had come up. Yet, now that the question was out, he realized that he'd been waiting for a chance to ask it.

"I haven't seen much of her," Jake said. He glanced sharply at his friend. "We don't exactly run in the same circles."

"No, I don't suppose you do. Not many people run in circles that exalted."

"Jenny never seemed to feel that way." Jake's dark eyes were curious. "You didn't say much when you left, but I got the feeling it had something to do with her."

"Something," was all Mitch offered. He shrugged. "It's all a long time ago. I just wondered how she was doing." He was sorry he'd brought up her name. Even after all these years, the memories could still get under his skin, as if the old wounds had never completely healed.

"She's doing all right, as far as I know. Seems to be pretty much running the Works, these days. Started there after her daddy's accident."

The accident. Would things have ended up the way they had if Willard Monroe hadn't wrecked his car that stormy night? The night he and Jenny had made love.

Mitch shrugged off the question. As he'd told Jake, it was all a long time ago. It no longer really mattered what might have happened. He'd spent enough time pondering what-ifs ten years ago. Jenny Monroe was nothing but a bittersweet memory. And he wanted to keep her that way.

Jenny tucked a stray lock of hair back into place, securing the immaculate chignon that gathered the honey-colored tresses at the back of her head. Beth was late, as usual, but she didn't mind. A few minutes alone were welcome, even if they were snatched in a coffee shop that bustled with lunchtime activity. At least, she wasn't expected to be a part of the bustle, she thought, leaning back against the booth.

Her feet ached and she longed to slip them out of the navy blue pumps she wore, but there was too much chance that someone would notice her stocking-clad feet under the table. Though she was not exactly a celebrity, there was generally a certain amount of discreet interest in her.

After all, her family's business was vital to the town's economy and people tended to be interested in what the Monroes were up to. Since her father rarely left the house these days and her mother was seldom seen in Ransome, Jenny tended to pick up more than her fair share of interest.

She sighed, wishing, for one disloyal moment, that she'd been born a Smith in a town that boasted a million people with that last name, instead of being a Monroe in a town that had reason to value the name. She squashed the thought as soon as it appeared. She had no reason to complain. She was healthy and still reasonably young, even if she occasionally felt closer to seventy-eight than twenty-eight.

"Am I late?" Beth slid into the booth opposite Jenny, breathless and flushed. "I had to finish a perm for Kathy. Her daughter's teacher called. Sara had just cut another little girl's braid's off—playing stylist, she said. The little girl's mother was having a fit, and Kathy had to go rescue Sara from the possibility of having revenge wrought on her six-year-old head. Kids. Whoever said they kept you young had obviously never had any of their own."

"And you wouldn't trade Mike and Adam for anything in the world," Jenny said, smiling at her friend.

"Oh, I don't know. If you offered me six weeks at a good spa, I might be tempted. You know, one of those places where they place the grapes between your lips and fan you with a palm frond."

"I think these days, they're more likely to get you up at five in the morning for a brisk hike and plunge you into ice baths than feed you grapes."

"Yech." Beth shuddered. "Whatever happened to good, old-fashioned hedonism?"

"It collided with the nineties and lost the war. So how are the Two Terrors?"

"Perfect, of course," Beth answered promptly. "Mike tried to drown Adam in his breakfast cereal this morning and Adam filled his father's best shoes with mud yesterday. Joe's convinced that both of them are changelings."

The waitress appeared and they gave her their orders. After she was gone, Beth leaned back against the padded booth and sighed.

"All kidding aside, I love those two, but it feels great to be away from them for a while."

"You're away from them at the salon," Jenny pointed out. She added a spoonful of sugar to her coffee and stirred it in.

"But then I have to deal with customers who are even worse than my two little terrors." She launched into a story about an eccentric client at the beauty salon where she worked part-time. Jenny listened and smiled at the appropriate places, but she couldn't help but wonder if Beth knew just how lucky she was.

Her home wasn't big and it was decorated in Early American Toddler, which meant that it was more practical than pretty, but it held a lot of love. Beth's husband adored her and she had two healthy, happy little boys.

Beth's story came to an end and Jenny laughed, forcing away the uncharacteristic mood. It wasn't as if she had any reason to feel sorry for herself, she reminded herself briskly.

"So, how's Bill?" Beth asked.

"Bill?" Jenny gave her a blank look.

"Bill Ramsey. The guy you're going to marry?" Beth prompted. "Jeez, Jenny, the least you could do was remember the guy's name."

"He's in New England on company business and I haven't forgotten his name," Jenny said, flushing. "I just wasn't thinking."

"Well, that's obvious. Otherwise, you wouldn't have gotten engaged to him." Beth didn't bother to try to conceal her disapproval of the relationship.

"I don't know why you don't like Bill. He's really very nice," Jenny fretted, wishing she could manage a more passionate defense.

"I've got nothing against Bill personally. I just object to you marrying someone you don't love."

"Who says I don't love him?" Jenny met Beth's look and shrugged, abandoning that line of defense. "Besides, we're not really engaged. We're just discussing the possibility right now."

"Jenny, you discuss the possibility of buying a new car or going on vacation. You *do not* discuss the possibility of marrying someone. At least you don't discuss it in the same way you'd discuss a . . . a merger of some sort."

In her determination to get her point across, Beth leaned across the table, her expression urgent. Jenny felt tears sting the backs of her eyes. There was no one else in her life who would argue so passionately against her marrying a perfectly nice man just because she wasn't in love with him. There was no one else who'd even recognize what she was—or in this case *wasn't*—feeling.

"Not everyone marries for love, Beth. Some people marry for companionship and . . . things."

"Ha." Beth's snort made her disgust plain. "You're a little young to be marrying for companionship. You're only thinking about marrying Bill because he's a good vice president and your father likes him."

"Doesn't *your* father like Joe?" Jenny asked defensively.

"Sure. But I'd have married him even if Dad hated his guts."

"Maybe you wouldn't feel that way if your father was in a wheelchair because of something you'd done," Jenny snapped.

"The accident wasn't your fault, Jenny. You didn't cause your father to lose control of his car."

"No. But he was looking for me, worried about me. And *that* was my fault."

"So you're going to spend the rest of our life trying to make up to him for it?"

It was an old argument, one they'd had many times over the past ten years. It wasn't possible for either to win. Nothing Beth could say would convince Jenny that she didn't bear a burden of responsibility for what had happened to her father ten years ago. And she certainly couldn't convince Beth that the guilt she felt was deserved.

With impeccable timing, the waitress appeared with their food. She set the plates on the table and asked if they needed anything else. Assured that they had everything they needed, she left, leaving a pool of silence behind her.

"Look, I'm sorry, Jenny." Beth spoke first, her expression worried. "I know I'm not going to be able to change your mind about the accident. It's just that I worry about you."

"I don't know why." Jenny picked up her fork and tried to look interested in the salad she'd ordered. "I'm doing fine. A lot of women would kill to have a job like mine. And though I know it's hard for you to believe, a lot of women would be glad to have a nice man like Bill Ramsey anxious to marry them."

"I never said Bill wasn't nice. I just don't think he's nice for you. You don't love him, Jenny."

"Love can grow," Jenny said stubbornly. She took a bite of her salad and chewed without interest.

"I suppose." Beth looked unconvinced, but Jenny was relieved to see that she seemed willing to drop the topic. Her relief, however, was destined to be short-lived.

"I talked to Mary Farmer yesterday," Beth said slowly.

"Whose reputation is she ripping to pieces this week?"

Mary Farmer had been a gossip when they were in high school together and she'd only gotten worse with age. If there was anything to be known about anybody, Mary was sure to ferret it out and tell thirty of her "closest friends."

"No one in particular, actually."

"Did you check her for fever?"

"I probably should have." Beth poked aimlessly at her own salad. It was obvious that something about her encounter with Mary had bothered her.

"Did Mary say something horrible about me?" Jenny asked, thinking that might be the source of her friend's distraction.

"No. Actually, she mentioned seeing someone you used to know."

"Really? Who?" Jenny looked at Beth with mild curiosity.

"Mitch Sullivan."

It was the last name she'd expected, and the impact of it showed on her face.

"Mitch?" She lifted one hand to her throat in an unconscious gesture of vulnerability.

"She said she saw him a couple of days ago." Beth's eyes were anxious. She, more than anyone, knew what Mitch had once been in Jenny's life. "She called around and found out that he's staying at the Lamplighter Motel."

"She called around?" Even through her shock, Jenny couldn't help but smile. "Thank God they haven't put her in charge of the FBI. None of us would ever have a trace of privacy again."

"I know. She's really unbelievable. But she's a fairly reliable source. If she says Mitch Sullivan is back in town, he's back in town."

"It's hard to believe," Jenny muttered. Catching Beth's worried eyes on her, she forced what she hoped was a convincing shrug. "I suppose that old saying about bad pennies always turning up must be true. I doubt he'll be around long."

"Probably not."

"Well, our paths aren't likely to cross," Jenny said lightly, smiling as if it were a matter of complete indifference to her.

Beth looked unconvinced, but when Jenny changed the subject, she was friend enough to go along with it. Afterward, Jenny couldn't have said what they talked about or what she ate. Though she always enjoyed her time with Beth, she was grateful when she could say that she had to get back to work.

But once in her car, she didn't immediately drive back to the factory. Instead, she drove out of town and parked on a quiet side road. Resting her hands on the

steering wheel, she stared out the windshield, oblivious to the mountains that filled the horizon in front of
her.

Mitch was back.

She hadn't thought of him in ages, at least not consciously. If she had given him any thought, she would
have told herself that she was long over him, that he
was part of her past, nearly forgotten. But her reaction to learning that he was back in Ransome made it
clear that she would have been lying to herself.

"Damn." She'd spent ten years learning to control
her emotions. She prided herself on the fact that she
never allowed emotion to get in the way of her business dealings. Only with her father and Beth were
feelings allowed to enter her life at all.

At eighteen, she'd learned the hard lesson of how
much emotion could cost a woman. After Mitch had
left town, she'd devoted herself to her father, doing
everything she could to make up to him the fact that
she'd been the cause of his accident. She'd been his
legs in those early days, little more than a messenger
service. He'd protested at first, but she'd been so in-
sistent that she wanted to help—needed to help—that
he'd given in.

After a while, he seemed to forget that she was still
young enough to have a life of her own. He'd simply
accepted that she was as involved with the business as
he was. Eventually it had become true. What had
started out as a way to expiate her guilt had become a
way of life. Jenny knew the business from the ground
up and she'd been making major decisions since she
was twenty-five.

The guilt was still there, but she'd learned to live with it. She sometimes thought that if her father had ever shown her any of the anger he must surely have felt, she could have begged his forgiveness and maybe put a little of the guilt behind her. But he'd never, by so much as a word or a look, made her feel as if he blamed her. He'd never reproached her for being with Mitch the night of the accident. He'd never even mentioned it to her. Paradoxically the fact that he didn't blame her only made her feel worse.

Sighing, Jenny leaned back against the soft leather seat and closed her eyes. Mitch. Just the name made memories roll over her. Mitch facing down Brad Louderman. Mitch telling her that a friendship would never work between them and then grudgingly agreeing to give it a try.

He'd been right, she thought, but she'd known that then. Friendship hadn't been what was on her mind. Her mouth curved in a rueful smile, remembering that younger, more confident Jenny. She'd been so sure she knew what she was doing. So sure she could handle Mitch Sullivan. She'd been such a little fool.

Shaking her head, she sat up and reached for the ignition key. It was all over a long time ago, and if she'd hadn't put it from her years ago, it was time to do so now. She had a business to run and she couldn't afford the time to dwell on ancient personal history.

Mitch's return to Ransome had nothing to do with her. As she'd told Beth, their paths weren't even likely to cross.

* * *

It was a Tuesday afternoon and the bank was not particularly busy. There had been two customers ahead of Mitch when he got in line, but one of them turned out to be an old man with a hearing problem who seemed to be attempting to deposit an unsigned check. The teller's repeated explanations didn't appear to make any particular impression.

Mitch guessed that it would have taken less time to rob the bank than it was taking to straighten out the old man's problems, but he was in no particular hurry. He'd finished a book the month before and he had no deadlines to meet for a while. And, one thing about writing, he could do it anywhere.

He glanced around the bank, giving half an ear to the teller's latest round of explanations and the old man's loudly voiced confusion. Too bad he didn't write comedy, he thought idly. He could have put this scene in a book. Of course, a little humor never hurt any—

Mitch lost track of the thought as his eyes fell on the woman leaving an office near the back of the bank. Her dark gold hair was pulled back from her face in a style as conservative as the pearl-gray suit she wore. It was a far cry from the jeans and knit tops he remembered, but he knew who she was. It came to him suddenly that he'd have known who she was if she'd been wearing a sack over her head.

Jenny.

Oblivious to the fact that the old man had finally left the window and the teller had turned an expectant look in his direction, Mitch moved toward Jenny.

She didn't notice him until he'd almost reached her, and he saw her eyes widen in shocked recognition.

"Hello, Jenny." He stopped in front of her.

"Mitch." The flat statement of his name revealed nothing of what she might be feeling. And after that first startled moment, her face had gone as cool and expressionless as her voice.

"It's been a long time."

"Yes."

"How have you been?"

"Fine." She seemed to realize that she was not really keeping up her end of the conversation. "How have you been?"

"Fine. Keeping busy."

His eyes went over her with a hunger that surprised him. She'd changed. And not altogether for the better. He hadn't expected to find the eighteen-year-old girl he'd known ten years ago. But it was more than age that had changed her.

She looked older than twenty-eight, closer to his own thirty-six. The hair he remembered as either tumbling to her shoulders or being pulled back in a saucy ponytail was scraped back from her face and drawn into a heavy twist at the back of her head. She wore not a trace of makeup and her skin seemed too pale, as if she spent too much time indoors. And the suit she wore, though clearly high quality, was so conservative it might have been called dowdy.

But it was the change in her eyes that struck him more than anything else. The soft chocolate color he remembered seemed darker, duller, somehow. And her eyes held none of the spark that had always seemed to be a little more alive than anyone around her.

"You've changed," he said, speaking half to himself. He wished the words back when he saw her shoulders stiffen.

"Most people do change in ten years."

"Sure. God knows, I feel more like a hundred years older." His tone was a little too hearty and he knew it. But he couldn't say anything more without adding insult to injury.

Damn. Open mouth, insert foot, why don't you, Sullivan?

"Are you staying in town long?" she asked, clearly making an effort at polite conversation.

"I don't know. My plans are loose, at the moment."

"That must be nice," she said in a tone that implied that he was a bum.

"I like it," he agreed, pretending the comment had been sincerely meant. "I'm helping Jake out at the garage while I'm in town," he said. "You remember Jake?"

"Of course. Someone told me he bought the garage a few years ago."

"Yeah."

They stared at each other as the awkward silence stretched between them. God, was this all they had left to say to each other?

"I'm sorry, but I have an appointment I need to get to." She gave him a polite smile that meant nothing. "It was nice to see you again, Mitch."

"Yeah. You, too." He turned to watch her walk away.

Jenny kept her spine rigidly straight, aware of his eyes on her every step of the way to the big glass doors at the front of the bank. She didn't relax her taut posture until she was safely enclosed in her car. Then she slumped over the wheel, feeling as if she'd just run a marathon.

Since Beth had told her that Mitch was back in town, she hadn't been able to get him out of her mind. For the past three days, she'd spent a lot of time looking over her shoulder, as nervous as a hunted criminal. When she hadn't seen him, she'd reminded herself that Ransome might not be a booming metropolis but it was hardly a tiny village, either. There was no reason on earth her path should cross that of Mitch Sullivan.

She hadn't been thinking about him at all when she'd come out of the bank president's office. Her thoughts had been strictly on business. And there he'd been.

He looked just the way she'd imagined he would. Older, a little harder perhaps. His hair was still the same inky black she remembered, still worn long enough to brush his collar. And his eyes... she'd almost managed to convince herself that she'd imagined the vivid blue of his eyes. But they were the way she remembered them, the color of a sapphire. And they still had the power to make her knees go weak.

That had just been shock, she told herself quickly. Shock had weakened her knees, nothing else.

From his expression, it was obvious that any shock he'd felt had been one of disappointment. "You've changed," he'd said. And not for the better, he might have added.

"I will not cry," she muttered oetween her teeth. She had to blink rapidly to banish the stinging in her eyes. She was not going to cry just because Mitch Sullivan thought she'd aged badly.

Had she really changed so much? She jerked down the visor, staring at her reflection in the lighted mirror there. The answer to her question stared back at her. It was hard to find even a trace of the girl she'd been ten years ago. Jenny wondered if she even existed anymore. Or had years of guilt and responsibility destroyed her forever?

"Idiot." She snapped the visor back into place and reached for the ignition key. What was she thinking of? Why should she care what Mitch Sullivan thought of how she looked? His opinion was a matter of complete indifference to her.

Of course he was disappointed in the changes he saw. It must have been obvious that she was no longer the silly little girl who'd hung on his every word. It didn't look as if he'd changed all that much. From the condition of the worn jeans and black T-shirt he'd worn, he was probably the same hell-raising, trouble-prone man he'd been.

The same man who'd left Ransome ten years ago. Who'd left *her* ten years ago.

Chapter 9

Jenny slid into the driver's seat and sat there, letting the day's tensions slide away. It was after nine o'clock and she'd been in her office since before eight in the morning. Around her, the parking lot was dark and empty. Everyone but the night guards had had the sense to go home hours ago. She probably should have done the same, but there didn't seem to be anything in particular to go home to. Especially since her mother had come back from San Francisco the night before.

That was one thing that hadn't changed over the years, she thought as she started the car. She and her mother still had absolutely nothing in common. It was sometimes hard to believe that they were even related, let alone mother and daughter.

Sighing, she pushed thoughts of Stephanie out of her mind. It was late and she was tired. She wanted a hot bath and a soft bed and about twelve hours of dreamless sleep.

She pulled out of the parking lot and turned the car's nose toward home. She was halfway there and starting to anticipate sliding into a tub of steaming water, when the engine stopped. There was no warning cough, no whine of protest. It simply stopped. Jenny steered it automatically toward the side of the road as it coasted to a standstill. Puzzled, she turned the key and was rewarded with a faint clicking noise but nothing more substantial.

"Great." She sat back in her seat and glared at the surrounding countryside—the *empty* countryside. She'd gotten in the habit of taking back roads home, finding the lack of traffic and more pleasant views compensated for the slightly longer drive. It was only now that it became clear that there were disadvantages to the route that she'd never considered. Like the fact that she was miles from the nearest phone or service station.

Muttering under her breath, she pushed open the door and stepped out onto the gravel shoulder. At least there was a full moon. She glanced up at the sky as she slung her purse over her shoulder and slammed the car door shut. At least she wasn't going to have to grope her way home on a moonless night.

Jenny struck out with long strides only to stumble on a fist-sized rock. Okay, so moonlight was a little deceptive. It was still better than no light. Modifying her pace, she moved down the road.

She'd been walking for less than ten minutes when she heard the sound of an engine approaching from behind. She hesitated a moment, debating the wisdom of trying to flag the driver down. Ransome didn't boast much crime but she *was* a woman, all alone on a deserted road at night. But the decision was taken out of her hands when the vehicle came around the curve in the road behind her. A headlight swept over her, illuminating her slim figure.

A motorcycle. Feeling a sense of déjà vu, Jenny stayed where she was as the big bike came to a stop in front of her. She felt no real surprise when she realized who had stopped. It seemed so natural. Sudden quiet fell as he shut off the engine.

"Mitch." Her eyes searched out the moonlight-shadowed angles of his face.

"Jenny." She couldn't see his eyes, but she could feel them going over her, from her knotted-back hair, over the plain navy suit to the matching pumps that had proved miserably unsuited to walking on a rough surface.

"I take it that was your car I passed about a mile back?"

"Only one mile?" she said, dismayed. "Is that all I've walked? It felt like at least ten."

"I bet it did. Those are hardly walking shoes."

He glanced at her pumps and Jenny was suddenly, inexplicably glad that she was wearing three-inch heels rather than the more practical low heels she generally wore. So what if she was damn near crippled from hiking along the road in them. They made the best of her slender legs.

"I hadn't planned on walking," she said.

"What's wrong with your car?" He brought his eyes back up to her face.

"It died."

"Now there's a good, technical explanation. The kind every mechanic dreams of hearing." His tone was teasing, and Jenny found the corners of her mouth turning upward.

Perhaps it was the darkness or the isolation, but she didn't feel the same tension she'd felt when she saw him at the bank two days ago. She didn't feel threatened by his presence, reminded of all the hurt she'd felt when he left. Instead, the conversation reminded her of the fun they'd had together.

"I could tell you that I think the whatchamacallit ate the thingamajig," she suggested.

"You could. But I'd have to tell you that it can't happen."

"Then, I guess you'll have to settle for 'it died.'"

"I guess I will." He was silent a moment and she felt his eyes on her face. "Get on."

The husky command sent a shiver up Jenny's spine. She stared at the hand he held out. Wasn't this how it had begun ten years ago? He'd come to her rescue on a moonlit road, given her a ride home and ended up breaking her heart.

She saw her hand go out without her conscious volition. His fingers closed over hers, strong and hard, the way she remembered them. This wasn't ten years ago, she reminded herself. She was older and wiser now. She was practically running a company. She'd come a long way from the foolish girl she'd been. So why did she suddenly feel as if she were eighteen again?

Jenny let Mitch help her onto the back of the bike, grateful that there was enough fullness in her skirt so that she didn't have to hike it all the way to her waist. Even so, once she was astraddle the bike, there was a considerable length of thigh exposed. She wasn't sure if she was sorry or glad that Mitch couldn't really see it.

"Hang on to my waist," he told her over his shoulder.

"I remember." She regretted the words immediately. The last thing she wanted to do was to remind either one of them of everything that had once passed between them. The stillness of Mitch's body told her that he was not immune to the memories any more than she was.

He started the bike without comment, and Jenny clutched at his waist as they moved off. She remembered the feeling of seeing the road fly by seemingly only inches away, remembered too, how incredibly secure she'd always felt as long as Mitch was driving. Within seconds, the wind had managed to whip her chignon loose from its pins. Feeling it tumble onto her shoulders, Jenny shook her head to loosen it completely. With the wind rushing through her hair, she felt suddenly younger and wilder. The responsible executive was swept away by the same wind that had loosened her hair.

Grinning foolishly, she tightened her hold on Mitch's waist and buried her face against his back. There was something about rushing down the road in the darkness, the wind in her hair, that made it impossible to think of the past or the future. Only the moment mattered.

When she felt the bike slow down, Jenny felt a pang of real regret. She didn't want the ride to end so soon. For a little while, she'd been able to forget the real world. But she could hardly ask Mitch to just keep driving.

He pulled up in front of her parents' house and cut the engine. The abrupt silence seemed almost painful. Or maybe what was painful was the feeling that reality was rushing in on her.

Jenny suppressed a sigh and sat up on the back of the bike, letting her hands slide away from his waist. The brief moment of forgetfulness was over. She wasn't eighteen anymore. She was a grown woman with the responsibilities to go with it. She slid awkwardly off the back of the bike and stood next to it, clutching her purse in front of her.

"Thanks for the ride."

"You're welcome."

She should turn and go into the house now, put an end to this chance meeting. But she lingered in the warm night air, feeling the pull of old memories.

"Brings back a lot of memories, doesn't it?"

It was hardly surprising that his thoughts paralleled her own. The similarity between tonight and ten years ago was too obvious to miss.

"Yes. It was a long time ago," she said regretfully.

"A long time," he agreed. It was impossible to read his expression in the moonlight, but his tone seemed to hold some of the same nostalgic regret that she felt.

Jenny felt an easing within her. In some odd way, it seemed as if they made a certain peace with each other in those few words. It helped to know that he also had regrets, that he hadn't just walked away and forgotten.

"You let your hair grow." Mitch reached out and caught a waist-length strand between his fingers. "It's beautiful."

"Thank you." But his next words doused the soft pleasure the compliment had given her.

"It's a shame to scrape it back all the time."

Jenny felt the fragile bubble of contentment burst. The word *scrape* made it sound as if what he was really saying was that she looked like an old woman. Dowdy and unattractive, just the way his eyes had made her feel when she'd seen him in the bank.

An annoyed flush rose in her cheeks and she jerked her head back, pulling the strand of hair from his fingers.

"How I wear my hair is none of your business," she snapped.

Spinning on her heel, she stalked up the steps and let herself into the house without a backward look.

Mitch watched her go, wishing he didn't have the niggling feeling that Jenny Monroe *was* his business.

"Jenny! What are you doing here in the middle of the afternoon?" Beth's face lit with pleasure as she saw who'd entered the salon. "Did they fire you?"

"No. I just decided to take a couple of hours off." Jenny glanced uneasily around the shop. "Are you busy? Do you have a customer waiting or something?''

"Nope. My two-o'clock appointment canceled about twenty minutes ago. I was thinking about going home early."

"Oh. Well, I don't want to keep you."

"You're not keeping me." Beth came out from behind the counter where she'd been temporarily manning the phone. "Is something wrong?"

"No." Jenny hesitated, gripping her purse so tightly that her knuckles turned pale. This was crazy. Why on earth had she even come here? Now she was going to have to think up some plausible excuse to give Beth as to why she'd dropped by in the middle of the afternoon.

"You look . . . funny," Beth said, peering into her friend's face. "Are you sure nothing's the matter."

"Of course not. I was just thinking about getting my hair cut." She forced a laugh to show that she knew the idea was foolish.

"You what?" Beth's voice rose on the question, drawing the attention of the receptionist who'd returned to her position behind the desk.

"It was a dumb idea," Jenny said, edging toward the door.

"Don't move." Beth clutched her arm to prevent her escape. "I'm not letting you out of here now."

"But I think I've changed my mind," Jenny protested as Beth dragged her further into the shop.

"You've come this far, Jen. It's bad luck to back out now."

"According to whom?" Jenny allowed herself to be pushed into a chair.

"According to me." Beth's fingers were already busy pulling out the pins that held Jenny's chignon in place, her expression gleeful. "I've been after you to let me chop off this mop for years."

"Do you have to use words like *chop?*" Jenny asked uneasily. In the mirror, she watched the heavy length tumble down. "I'm not sure about this, Beth."

"Too late," Beth told her. "I'm not letting you go now."

She lifted handfuls of thick honey-gold hair, eyeing Jenny's reflection in the mirror with much the same concern a entomologist would give a particularly interesting species of beetle. Seeing her expression, Jenny surrendered to the inevitable.

"Did you have anything in mind?" Beth asked absently, drawing Jenny's hair back to study the shape of her face.

Something that would make Mitch Sullivan sit up and take notice, was Jenny's first response, quickly suppressed. Her decision to get her hair cut had absolutely nothing to do with Mitch's words the night he'd given her a ride home. Just because she hadn't been able to get the word *scrape* out of her head for two days didn't mean that was why she was getting it cut. She was just making a considered choice, that's all.

"Something young and sassy," she said, staring at her reflection. "And easy to take care of," she added, making a quick gesture toward practicality.

Beth's round face creased in a delighted smile and she all but rubbed her hands together in anticipation.

"You won't regret this, Jen. You're going to look fantastic."

Jenny half thought she might already regret it, but she wasn't going to change her mind now.

An hour later, she stared at her reflection, hardly recognizing the woman who looked back at her. The heavy length of hair was gone, replaced by a layered cut that didn't quite reach her shoulders. The shorter length released the natural curl she'd forgotten she had and her hair looked artfully tumbled.

"It looks lighter," she said, seeing the light catch on golden highlights she'd never seen before.

"That's because of the layering. It catches the light more." Beth stood back to survey her work, looking smug. "What do you think?"

"It doesn't look like me anymore," Jenny said, eyeing the stranger in the mirror uneasily.

"Yes, it does. Your *old* hair was what didn't look like you. You've been hiding under that hair, Jenny, and it was smothering you. This lets the real you come out."

"You make it sound like I've just gone through therapy."

"Don't kid yourself. A new haircut is some of the best therapy around."

"I don't know. It doesn't look very businesslike, does it?" Jenny gathered the new, shorter length into her hands and started to pull it up on top of her head. "Ow!"

She dropped her hair as Beth reached out to slap her hands. Her startled gaze met her friend's in the mirror.

"Don't you dare try to bundle it back into a bun," Beth said fiercely, looking not in the least apologetic at having resorted to physical violence.

"But I have to look like a businesswoman," Jenny protested.

"This is the nineties, not the thirties, and you don't have to look like a drudge to get respect."

"Maybe you're right." Jenny turned her head experimentally, watching her hair swing around her face. It really did make her look younger, softer. A long way from having it "scraped" back from her face.

Maybe she'd drop by Eddie's Garage. Mitch had said he was working there while he was in town. After all, it wouldn't hurt to thank him for giving her a lift home the other night.

"You've got a visitor, Mitch." Jake's words gave Mitch the feeling of having fallen into a time warp. The longer he was in Ransome, the stronger the feeling had grown and the announcement, so familiar ten years ago, seemed the final evidence that the past ten years had been nothing but a dream.

He pulled his head out of the engine compartment and reached automatically for the rag he'd stuck in his back pocket. He didn't even feel any real surprise when he saw Jenny hovering at the front of the garage. It couldn't have been anyone else.

Walking toward her, he half expected to see the same jeans-clad girl he'd fallen in love with. But she was wearing another of the suits that seemed to constitute her uniform these days. This one was pale pink, but that was the only real difference between it and the others, as far as he could tell.

"Hi."

"Hi." Jenny was suddenly sure that this was a mistake. Hadn't she learned her lesson ten years ago? Didn't she have sense enough to keep her distance from Mitch Sullivan?

"What can I do for you?" Mitch asked, and her mind promptly went completely blank. She cleared her throat, forcing herself to remember why she'd come.

"I just wanted to thank you for giving me a lift the other night. I wasn't sure I remembered to do so at the time."

"You remembered."

His eyes wandered over her, settling on the new haircut. Jenny forced herself not to reach up and fuss with it. Her chin lifted defensively. If he thought she'd cut it because of what he'd said . . . But all he did was smile, and the appreciative look in his eyes started a warm glow in the pit of her stomach. It had been a long time since she'd seen that look in a man's eyes.

Not that she cared whether or not he approved of her new haircut, she reminded herself hastily.

"Get your car fixed?" he asked.

"Yes. There was something wrong with something."

"Ah, the old something-wrong-with-something problem. That's a tough one."

She couldn't help but return his teasing smile. The warm glow grew stronger, warning her. Mitch had always been able to make her feel this way. But it hadn't lasted.

Mitch wondered what had happened to cause her smile to fade, replaced by the cool mask that seemed to be so much a part of her these days. When she smiled, she looked almost like the girl he'd known. She glanced at her watch.

"Well, I should be going. I have a meeting to get to."

"You seem to have a lot of meetings these days," he said, reminding her that she'd said the same thing the day they'd met in the bank.

"Since my father's accident I've done my best to take as much of the burden of the company from him as possible."

"I didn't realize your father was ill," Mitch said.

"He's paralyzed," Jenny said, as if that explained everything.

"Yes, I know." Mitch debated pursuing the topic, asking her why her father's paralysis meant he couldn't run his company, but he decided to let it drop. For all he knew, Willard Monroe had never adjusted to his condition and had withdrawn from life.

"Well, I'd better get going," Jenny said again. She gave him a half smile that failed to disturb the stillness of her features.

"See you around."

Mitch stood where he was and watched until her car slid out of the parking lot. What had happened in her life to drive all the life from her eyes?

And why the hell should it matter to him?

Chapter 10

There was, as always, a line in front of the counter at Gloria's Glorious Sandwich shop. Saturday afternoons were particularly busy. She'd been foolish to think she could just run in and grab a sandwich and run back out, Jenny realized.

All Gloria's Glorious Sandwiches were named after celebrities, but that was just the gimmick to persuade people to try them the first time. After that, no one needed any persuasion to come back.

Glancing at the numbered ticket in her hand and then up at the digital display on the back wall, she calculated that there were fifteen people ahead of her. At this rate, she'd get a meal faster if she drove to Denver for it, she thought, irritated.

She crumpled the ticket and tossed it into the trash as she turned to leave. Before she reached the door, a familiar voice called her name.

She felt a shiver go up her spine as she turned to face Mitch. But it was a shiver of anticipation, she acknowledged uneasily, not the dislike she should have felt. Or, even better, indifference.

"Giving up?" he asked, nodding to the crowd in front of the counter.

"Well, I thought it would be nice to eat sometime in this century."

"But where else could you eat a sandwich like Gloria's?"

"Nowhere. That's why they're so busy." She shrugged. "I was just going to pick up something and take it back to the office, anyway. It doesn't really matter what it is."

"I happen to have a ticket only three numbers away." Mitch gave her a considering look. "I could be persuaded to add your order to mine."

"Wouldn't that be cheating? Sort of like cutting in line?"

"You think all these people are only ordering sandwiches for themselves? Half the town is probably skulking in the back alley, waiting for their lunch."

"Skulking?" Damn him. How was it he always managed to make her smile? Even when she was determined to keep her distance, he still managed to slip under her guard. "I doubt if there are many people in Ransome who skulk."

"You'd be surprised what people will do for food as good as this. So, what do you want?"

Jenny glanced at the crowd and looked back at Mitch. "Well, I was going to get a Mickey Rooney."

"Mickey Rooney?" He winced. "I was going to order a Mae West. The thought boggles the mind."

"Since we're not going to eat together, I don't think it matters."

"You haven't heard my condition yet."

"Condition," she questioned warily. "What condition?"

"The one that has to be met before I agree to use my influence to get your lunch."

"Having a lower number isn't exactly 'influence,'" she said dryly. "What's the condition?"

"Have lunch with me."

The suggestion surprised her and her refusal was automatic. "I can't. I told you, I was just going to take a sandwich to the office and do some work."

"Is there anything that has to be done today?"

"Well, no," she admitted slowly.

"Then have lunch with me. We'll take our sandwiches and picnic somewhere."

"I'm not really dressed for a picnic," she said, indicating her floral cotton skirt and the soft white shirt she wore with it.

"Looks good to me. No excuses. If you want your Mickey Rooney, you're going to have to put up with my company."

"It's not you," she protested automatically, though they both knew it was a lie. She suspected he even knew that it was certainly not dislike that made her hesitate.

"Fifty-two." One of the women behind the counter called out the number, looking for the holder of ticket number fifty-two.

"That's me," Mitch said, his eyes holding Jenny's. "Should I order your sandwich?"

"That's blackmail," she protested.

"Fifty-two," the woman called again.

"I takes my opportunities where I sees them," he said in a fair Popeye voice.

"Last call. Fifty-two."

Jenny threw a harassed look over Mitch's shoulder to where the woman waited, her expression impatient.

"Scared?" he asked, raising one brow in arrogant challenge.

"All right," she said, knowing she was probably making a mistake.

"Here." Mitch spun toward the counter, holding up his ticket. "Sorry."

Jenny hung back, watching him order their sandwiches and wondering if she'd lost her mind.

Half an hour later, she was sure of it when she realized where Mitch planned on having their picnic. She eased her foot off the gas as she saw Mitch's bike take the turn to Falune Hill. She hadn't been on Falune Hill since the last time she'd gone there with Mitch. Fourth of July, ten years ago, to be exact.

He couldn't have forgotten what had happened there, which meant he had to have chosen this location deliberately. Jenny hesitated. There was nothing to stop her from turning her car around and going back the other way. Of course, he had the sandwiches, insurance against her changing her mind, he'd admitted up front.

But not even a sandwich from Gloria's was worth the emotional turmoil she sensed waiting for her at the top of that hill. On the other hand, it she turned tail and ran, that would be like admitting to herself—and to him—that what had happened all those years ago still affected her.

Scared? The challenge echoed in her mind. Of course she wasn't scared of him or anything else. Muttering under her breath, Jenny turned the car onto the dirt road that wound its way up the back of the hill.

Everything was just the same as she remembered. It had been a fairly wet summer so far and the grass was still green, though it was starting to look a little tired. There was the same panoramic view from the top of the hill. Ransome looked like a toy town from here. And the silence was absolute.

Jenny got out of her car and opened the trunk to get the blanket she kept there for emergencies. When she'd put it there, she'd been thinking more along the lines of having the car stall on a snowy road. But it would serve just as well for an impromptu picnic.

If Mitch had had an ulterior motive for choosing this particular spot for their meal, there was no sign of it in his expression as she approached. He stood on the thick layer of needles that covered the ground under a huge old pine.

"I used to think of this view when I was in Europe," he said as she stopped a little ways from him. Jenny followed his eyes to the panorama spread beneath them, the horizon seemingly forever away.

"You can see forever," he said, unconsciously echoing her own thoughts. "Sometimes it was hard to remember just what forever looked like."

"So you made it to Europe," she said, her voice holding a slightly wistful note.

"I made it to Europe," he confirmed.

Turning, he took the blanket from her and spread it on the pine needles where the tree branches would shade them from the hot afternoon sun. Setting the sack from Gloria's in the middle of the blanket, he settled on one side of the blanket.

Jenny hesitated before sinking down across from him. If he'd brought her up here to remind her of old times, she couldn't tell it from his behavior. She didn't believe he'd forgotten the Fourth of July they'd spent here, so she could only think he was trying to show her that he wasn't trying to dredge up old memories.

She reached for the sandwich he was holding out, feeling herself start to relax. Maybe she hadn't been so foolish to agree to this after all.

They didn't talk much at first, but the silence was not uncomfortable. Jenny would never have believed that sharing a meal with Mitch could be a pleasant, undemanding experience. Considering all that lay between them, it didn't seem as if they should be able to share a meal without every minute being filled with the tensions of old memories.

"How long did you spend in Europe?" Jenny asked as she picked up the second half of her sandwich.

"Almost two years."

"Was it everything you'd hoped?"

"Well, it wasn't exactly the romantic Europe of Hemingway's time," he said ruefully. "But it had its charms."

"What about your writing?" She set the untouched half a sandwich back in its wrapper.

"I kept up with it," Mitch said.

Thinking that it might be a sensitive topic, Jenny didn't pursue the subject of his dream of being a writer. It seemed obvious that he hadn't known great success or he probably wouldn't be back in Ransome, working for Jake.

"Tell me about Europe," she said instead. Drawing her knees up under her full skirt, she wrapped her arms around them.

"It was very...European," Mitch said. Catching her disgusted look, he grinned. "All right. What do you want to know?"

"Does it really rain all the time in England? Are French women really more chic than American women? Is Stonehenge as spectacular as it looks in pictures? Did you see the Parthenon? Did you run with the bulls in Barcelona?"

"Hold on." Grinning, Mitch held up a hand in protest and Jenny subsided, blushing as she realized that she probably sounded like an overeager teenager. But she'd had so little chance to travel.

"Let me see if I can answer these in order." Frowning in concentration, he ticked the answers off on his fingers. "All the time. I didn't notice. Even more so. Yes and it's incredible. And hell, no."

"I've forgotten the questions," Jenny admitted.

Their eyes met and the laughter couldn't be contained. Listening to her soft laugh, Mitch felt as if he'd come home. For ten years, he'd been waiting to hear that sound again and he hadn't even known it.

The laughter served to banish any lingering tension that remained and the conversation flowed easily from there. It consisted largely of Mitch talking about the places he'd seen, with Jenny prompting him with questions.

Listening to him talk, it was obvious that he'd spent most, if not all the time since he'd left Ransome, traveling. It seemed to Jenny as if he'd been everywhere. He'd spent six months in Australia, three in Africa. And when he wasn't in some exotic part of the world, he'd apparently traveled all over the United States.

Whether he'd made a success of his writing or not, he certainly had a gift for description. She felt as if she had only to close her eyes to see the people and places he was talking about.

"Enough about me," he said finally. He was sitting on the blanket, one knee drawn up, an elbow resting on it. "I haven't talked so much about myself in all my life. I must sound like an egomaniacal bore."

"I enjoy hearing about the places you've seen," Jenny protested. "I'd think with your ability to describe things, that you ought to be able to sell travel articles. Have you tried some of the magazines that specialize in that sort of thing?"

Mitch gave her a startled look, seeing the helpful concern in her eyes. She was trying to encourage him not to give up on his dream, he thought. The fact that it wasn't necessary didn't make her concern any less touching.

"I'll give it some thought," he mumbled. "What about you? What about your plans to go into nursing?"

"Nursing?" Jenny was startled by the reminder of that old dream. It had been a long time since she'd even given it any thought. "Oh, that was a silly idea. I gave that up years ago."

"Why?"

"Why?" How did you explain the death of a dream? "Well, after Daddy came home from the hospital, I became his go-between from home to the office. Mostly, I ran papers back and forth and tried to make sure that things ran smoothly."

"I would have thought you were a little young for that," Mitch commented.

"I didn't do too badly. I learned quickly." There was a touch of pride in the admission. "Of course, it was a long time before I was making any important decisions in the company. Even now, Daddy's still the one in charge."

"So, he's still involved in the day-to-day running of the Works?" Mitch was probing, trying to build a picture of her life over the past ten years.

"Not exactly. He rarely comes into the office, of course. I handle most of the day-to-day stuff myself, trying to keep as much of the burden off him as possible."

There it was again. That implication that Willard Monroe had hidden himself away from the world after the accident. It didn't fit with the image he'd had of the man.

"How did your father cope with being paralyzed?" he asked, deciding to just ask what he wanted to know.

"Amazingly well, really." Jenny pressed her cheek to her updrawn knees, her expression pensive in the sunlight that filtered through the pine boughs above them. "He never complained, not even in the beginning."

Mitch had to bite back the urge to ask why, if he'd coped so well, he'd thrown the burden of running his business on an eighteen-year-old girl's shoulders.

"Do you like being an executive in the family business, nursing a bunch of dining room furniture instead of a ward full of patients?" he asked with a smile.

"It has its moments," she said.

He wondered if she even heard her own lack of enthusiasm. "I'd guess the boards complain less than the patients would," he said lightly.

"That's true. Besides, I suspect I wouldn't have made a very good nurse anyway."

"I'd let you bandage my wounds any day." He'd intended the comment to sound comically lascivious. But somewhere between intention and reality, it changed, coming out on a husky note that didn't sound at all comical.

As easy as that, the sexual awareness that was never far from the surface between them was suddenly a very real presence. Their eyes locked and the sunny afternoon faded away. There was nothing and no one in the world but the two of them, alone on their very own hilltop.

Jenny's eyes widened as Mitch leaned toward her. She should move away, she thought. She couldn't just sit here as if she *wanted* him to kiss her.

And then his mouth touched hers and she stopped thinking. She nearly stopped breathing. The kiss was hardly more than a gentle brushing of his mouth over hers.

Mitch drew back and looked at her, a question in his eyes she couldn't even begin to understand, let alone answer. All she knew was that she wanted him to kiss her again. Perhaps he read that in her eyes. Or perhaps he was simply following his own desire. Jenny didn't care which it was as long as he was kissing her again.

She lifted her head to meet him this time, her hands coming up to find the broad strength of his shoulders, clinging there as his mouth opened over hers. His tongue swept into her mouth, finding hers, claiming her for his.

All the passion was still there. It was as if the ten years that had passed between their last kiss and this one had only allowed the hunger to grow stronger. Mitch kissed her as if he were a starving man and she was the most delicious feast he'd ever seen. He devoured her mouth, melting every bone in her body.

This was what he'd been missing for ten years, Mitch thought. His arms came around her, easing her back onto the blanket until they were pressed together from chest to thigh. This was the one thing he'd never been able to find in all his travels.

There had never been any other woman who completed him the way Jenny did. It was like finding the other half of his soul. He slid his hands under her, arching her up against his chest, feeling the soft pressure of her breasts through the layers of their clothing.

He wanted to strip the annoying barriers away and make love to her on the sun-dappled blanket. He wanted to show her with his body, all the things he was feeling, all the hunger and need that had burned in him for ten years.

But a small voice intruded, telling him that he'd be making the mistake of his life. If he rushed her, he was going to lose her again. And despite the fact that she was pliant in his arms, that her mouth was as hungry as his, something told him that to make love to her now would be a mistake.

Mitch wanted to ignore the voice of reason. His fingers curled into her hair, his mouth slanting almost roughly over hers as he sought to quench a ten-year thirst.

Jenny was no less demanding. From the moment his mouth touched hers, she'd slammed the door on the warning bell that suggested she was asking for trouble. She didn't want to hear that this was the same man who'd shattered her heart. She didn't want to think about all the good, responsible arguments against behaving the way she was behaving.

All she wanted was the feel of Mitch's body on hers, the taste of him on her tongue. She buried her fingers in his hair, drawing him closer, wanting to somehow absorb him into herself.

When Mitch started to pull away, she moaned softly in protest.

"Jenny." Her name was a husky groan against her mouth as he gave into the temptation to kiss her again. He could never get enough of her. But if he didn't stop now, he was going to ruin any chance of getting back what they'd once had. It was too soon. His mind knew that, even while his body screamed that it wasn't too soon at all.

"This is getting out of hand," he muttered finally, dragging his mouth from hers.

Jenny stared up at him, her hands still linked behind his head, her eyes chocolate brown and full of a dazed need that made Mitch curse his own common sense.

"Jenny..." He wanted to talk to her, to see if she felt any of the same things he did. But before he could say anything more than her name, the dazed look vanished, to be replaced by complete mortification.

"Oh, my God," she whispered. She jerked her hands away from him and pressed them against her burning cheeks. "What have I done?"

"Nothing. Jenny, this was inevitable."

But she wasn't listening. She pushed frantically at his shoulders and Mitch sat up, allowing her room to do the same. She brushed her skirt over her knees, her hands shaking.

Mitch gave her the space she seemed to need, but when she started to get up, he reached out to catch her arm, stopping her.

"Jenny, we need to talk."

"I have to go," she muttered without looking at him.

He recognized the futility of trying to talk to her now. She was too upset. "But I want to see you again."

She shot him a quick look, giving him a glimpse of the turmoil she was feeling. She shook her head, not so much refusing him as denying her own confusion.

"I don't know," she whispered. Without giving him time to respond, she pulled away from his loose hold and scrambled to her feet.

Mitch stayed where he was, watching her all but run for the safety of her car. She might not know, but he did. If he had to move heaven and earth to do it, he'd see her again. This time, there would be no unfinished business between them.

For almost a week, Jenny avoided Mitch's calls. He called her at home the day after their picnic. He called her at the office on Monday. Tuesday he called twice at the office and once at home in the evening. Wednesday there were four calls to the office but none at home. Thursday there was only one call and Friday not even that.

Jenny holed up in her office and tried to pretend that she was working. She didn't know if she was fooling anyone else, but *she* knew she was accomplishing nothing. Unless you counted bending innumerable paper clips into tortured shapes and watching the phone as if it might turn into a cobra at any moment.

By Friday evening, she was undecided as to which was worse: having Mitch call several times a day or having him not call at all. The last call had been yesterday morning, she thought, staring at the stack of untouched paperwork on her desk. Not a word since then.

What if he'd left town again?

She closed her eyes against the shaft of pain caused by that thought. Well, so what if he had? Wasn't that exactly what she'd been expecting since he returned? Wasn't that why she'd been determined not to let herself get involved with him again?

Again? Who was she kidding? When *hadn't* she been involved with Mitch Sullivan? From the moment he'd come back to Ransome, she'd been involved. And if she was completely honest with herself, she couldn't really say that she'd ever been *uninvolved* even while he was gone.

She sighed and stood, giving up even the pretense of working. It was almost ten o'clock. She usually liked being at work when the building was empty and everything was still. But tonight it only served to remind her of how alone she was.

She turned off her office light on the way out. Walking through the quiet building, it struck her suddenly that she'd been a fool to avoid Mitch's calls. What if he'd left town? She'd let her fear of the emotions he roused dominate her thinking. And she'd pushed him away when all she really wanted was to hold him close.

Feeling tears sting the backs of her eyes, she pushed open the front door and stepped out into the empty parking lot. The door closed with a heavy whoosh behind her, locking automatically. Jenny's car was parked near the entrance, sitting in lonely splendor beneath a light. The light gleamed off the shiny blue paint. It also revealed, with depressing clarity, the two flat tires on the passenger side.

Jenny stopped cold and stared at the tires. They'd been fine this morning. Kids, she thought. Kids playing a stupid prank. And now, here she was stuck in an empty parking lot in the middle of the night. For a moment, she was too depressed to even think of the obvious, which was that all she had to do was have one of the night guards let her back in. Then she could call a cab to take her home.

For the moment, the empty parking lot and the flat tires seemed like some kind of metaphor for her life. And then she heard a husky and oh-so-familiar voice behind her.

"Need a ride, lady?"

"Mitch." She hardly breathed his name as she turned toward the sound of his voice. *He hadn't gone!* That one thought dominated all others.

"Looks like you're in need of a ride." He was leaning against the Harley, standing just beyond the circle of light. Wearing black jeans and a soft black shirt, he was little more than a deeper shadow against the dark building behind him.

"I guess I do," she said, moving slowly toward him.

"Your chariot awaits." He straightened and swept one hand toward the bike.

"Well, it's got two wheels. I guess that qualifies it as a chariot." She hardly knew what she was saying.

She could feel the pulse in her throat beating much too fast and hard.

Without another word, Mitch helped her onto the bike. Jenny felt, more than saw, the way his eyes lingered on the length of thigh exposed by her skirt. She tugged nervously at the hem.

If she was going to get in the habit of riding a motorcycle, she was going to have to start wearing clothes more suited to it, she thought. Of course, there was no reason to think she was going to get a chance to make a habit of this sort of thing.

Mitch slid onto the bike in front of her and lifted it upright, nudging the kickstand up. Jenny put her arms around his waist and pressed her face against his back. He seemed to hesitate a moment as if her action surprised him, but he didn't say anything. The roar of the motorcycle's engine echoed off the building, filling the empty parking lot with thunderous sound.

Surely one of the nicest things about motorcycles was the fact that they made conversation all but impossible, Jenny thought. If Mitch had been driving a car, she'd be trying to think of something to say to fill the silence. But perched on the back of the Harley, her arms wrapped tight around his waist, her cheek pressed against the strong muscles of his back, there were no polite social conventions to observe.

Absorbed in her thoughts, Jenny paid no attention to their route. It wasn't until she felt the bike slow and turn off the road that she lifted her head and realized that he hadn't brought her home. A white neon sign announced that they were at the Lamplighter Motel. A yellow neon flame dotted the *i*.

Mitch pulled into a parking place and cut the engine. Neither of them moved or spoke for a moment, and then he slid off the bike and turned to offer his hand to her. Jenny hesitated, looking from his hand to the motel.

"We need to talk, Jenny."

"Just talk?" she questioned.

"If that's all you want."

His words would have been more reassuring if she'd been a little more sure about what she wanted.

She should insist that he take her home, she thought, staring at the hand he was offering to take. But for the first time in ten years, she was starting to feel really alive again. Beth was always telling her that she was too cautious, that she needed to kick over the traces and live a little. She suspected that Beth would approve heartily of her taking Mitch's hand.

Her instincts, so often ignored, were telling her that this wasn't the time to take the safe road. It was time to take a few risks, live a little dangerously.

Feeling as if she were about to walk into the lion's den completely unarmed, Jenny set her trembling fingers in Mitch's and let him pull her off the bike.

Chapter 11

Mitch's room was not fancy, but there was a certain comfort in its anonymous cream walls and plain furnishings. There were a few signs of Mitch's occupancy that made it a little less impersonal. A pair of jeans was draped across the arm of a chair. A running shoe lay on its side in front of the closet door.

"How about a glass of wine?" Mitch said. He tossed his keys onto the table next to the bed and turned to look at Jenny, who continued to hover close to the door, as if she still hadn't quite decided to stay.

"I don't think so," she said, thinking that wine was the last thing she needed at the moment. On the other hand, a little wine might settle the butterflies in her stomach. "Actually, that sounds nice."

Mitch didn't seem to think there was anything odd about her abrupt change of mind. He pulled open the top drawer of the dresser and took out a bottle and two glasses.

"It's a cabernet," he said as he picked up a corkscrew. "I've never developed a taste for white wines."

"Cabernet is fine," she told him. At the moment, she was so nervous that she wouldn't be able to tell the difference between a fine cabernet and cheap jug wine.

While he was opening the wine, she wandered over to the table that sat in front of the window. The curtains were drawn now, but she guessed that, during the day, the window would provide plenty of light. There were several notepads lying on the table, the top sheet of each filled with handwriting. A notebook computer sat in the center of the table. Having just looked into the possibility of buying a few ultraportable computers for the company, Jenny's brows rose. A pricey little piece of equipment.

Curious, she picked up the nearest notepads and scanned the top sheet. Her interest was immediately caught. What she was holding appeared to be the beginning of a novel—a very good novel, she thought, if it was possible to judge from the opening. In the first line the hero was thrown from a moving train somewhere in Europe. Dazed and injured, he stumbled to a farmhouse where an elderly couple took him in. The writing was crisp and vivid, painting the picture in a few quick words, and she felt as if she could see the scene that was being described.

Jenny flipped to the next page, so absorbed in what she was reading that she didn't hear Mitch come up behind her.

"Your wine."

Startled, she dropped the tablet back onto the table and turned to face him, a guilty flush coloring her cheeks.

"I'm sorry. I shouldn't have been snooping."

"They're not top secret," he said, shrugging. "Snoop all you want."

"It looks very exciting." She took the wineglass from him.

"Good. It's supposed to."

"Do you have a publisher for it?"

"Yeah." He sipped his wine and slanted her an unreadable look from under his lashes. "The same one who published my last book."

"Your last book?" Jenny had started to lift her glass to her mouth, but she lowered it and stared at him. "You've published a book?"

"Actually, this will be number five. It should be out next year sometime."

"Have I heard of you? I mean, what name do you write under?"

"M.L. Sullivan."

Jenny's eyes widened in recognition. "I've seen your books!"

"Good. That's the idea of having them published," Mitch said.

"But . . . but you're really successful, aren't you?"

He grinned at her phrasing, at the surprise in her voice. "I've done fairly well."

"But you said . . ." She stopped, her brows coming together in a frown as she tried to remember just what he *had* said. Had he said anything at all or had she just assumed he hadn't attained his dream of selling his writing? "Why didn't you tell me?"

"I don't know." He shrugged. "It didn't seem all that relevant."

"You must have thought I was pretty funny, encouraging you to send articles to travel magazines." She flushed, remembering her helpful words of advice.

"I thought you were very sweet," he corrected. He reached out and brushed his fingers over her flushed cheek. "You were encouraging me to reach for my dream."

Jenny wanted to be annoyed with him for not telling her the truth about his writing. She knew she should feel as if he'd made a fool out of her and she should resent it. But the expression in his eyes wasn't saying she was foolish. She looked away, not sure she was ready to see what was in his eyes.

"So, what brought you back to Ransome?" she asked as she moved away from the table and, not incidentally, away from Mitch. She felt as if she needed some breathing space. But his next words suspended her breath.

"You brought me back."

"What?" Jenny spun to face him, her eyes wide and startled.

"You were the reason I came back," he said, his gaze steady on hers.

"Me?" she whispered, her voice stolen by surprise. "You came back because of me?"

"There's a lot of unfinished business between us, Jenny. I think you know it as well as I do."

"I don't know what you're talking about," she denied.

She shouldn't have come in with him, she thought. She wasn't ready for this, wasn't ready for *him*. She wasn't sure she'd ever be ready. She looked around for a place to set her wineglass, but Mitch solved the problem for her.

"I'm talking about this," he said. He swept one arm around her waist, dragging her up against his hard frame. Jenny cried out, startled, when he wound his free hand in her hair and tilted her head back. She had a fleeting glimpse of his eyes, stormy blue and determined and then his mouth came down on hers.

The wineglass tilted and then dropped from her fingers, spilling bloodred wine across the carpet. They neither noticed nor cared.

Jenny's hands hovered over Mitch's shoulders for an instant, as if debating whether to push him away, but there was never any real question of that. She could no more push him away than she could swim the English Channel. She wanted this as much as he did, needed it as much as she needed air.

Her mouth opened beneath the demand of his as her fingers slipped into the thick darkness of his hair. She rose on tiptoe, molding herself more firmly against him.

There was a certain desperation in the kiss when it began, as if he had to prove something to both of them. But his hold gentled and the desperation eased when he felt Jenny's reaction, tasted it in the eager response of her mouth and the soft curve of her body against his.

Just when Jenny was starting to think the kiss would never end, he lifted his head, but he didn't move away. He leaned his forehead against hers. Jenny kept her eyes closed, listening to the rough sound of his breathing and feeling as if she'd be content to stay in his arms forever.

"That's why I came back," Mitch said raggedly. "Even after ten years, it's still there."

"Yes." She hardly knew what she was agreeing to. But she knew that she never felt as complete anywhere else as she did in Mitch's arms.

"Why did you send me away, Jenny?" His voice was laced with old pain.

"I never thought you'd go." Jenny drew back until she could meet his eyes. "I was so confused, Mitch. And so guilty. I thought I owed it to my father to break up with you. That's why I told you I didn't want to see you anymore that day at the garage. But, deep down, I never really believed you'd go. I didn't think you'd believe me."

"I didn't. Not at first." His hands dropped away from her and he stepped back, shaking his head. "I knew you were upset about your father's accident."

"But you still left." Jenny wrapped her arms around her waist in an unconscious attempt to banish the chill she felt, remembering those bleak days after he'd gone.

"Only after you refused to see me." He shoved his hands into his pockets as if the memories brought the same chill to him. "Your mother made it perfectly clear that you wanted to have nothing more to do with me."

"My mother?" Confused, she shook her head. "What did my mother have to do with it?"

"I came to your house."

"I know. And you left without bothering to see me."

"You didn't bother to come downstairs," he shot back, his voice sharp with remembered hurt.

"By the time I got downstairs, you'd gone," she cried, her eyes filling with tears. "Mother said you'd come to say goodbye because you were leaving for Europe. I wanted to die." The last words were a whisper.

"I wasn't leaving for Europe. I didn't make it to Europe for almost a year. I didn't have enough money, yet."

"But you were gone. I drove by the garage every day for almost a month and I didn't see you. If you didn't go to Europe, why did you leave?"

"I left because I didn't want to be in this town, where there was a chance of running into you. I didn't think I could stand that." He half turned away from her, thrusting his fingers through his hair. "I just wanted out."

"But she told me you'd gone to Europe," Jenny said, shaking her head. "If you didn't say that's where you were going, why did she say that?"

"I don't know. Maybe because it sounded about as far away as possible." He shrugged. "It doesn't matter now. Why wouldn't you see me, Jenny? Why did you ask your mother to talk to me?"

"Why did I . . ." Jenny's voice trailed off and she stared at him, her eyes stricken as she began to see what must have happened. "Oh, God." She lifted her hand to her mouth, her fingers trembling. "Oh, God."

"What is it?"

"She lied, Mitch. Oh, God, she lied." She closed her eyes as a single tear spilled over and wound its way slowly down her cheek. She opened her eyes in time to see understanding dawn on his face.

"And I believed her," he said slowly.

"I didn't know you were there. I was in the shower. When I heard your bike leaving, I ran downstairs. And she told me you'd come to say goodbye."

"But she knew things," Mitch protested. He was having a difficult time accepting that Stephanie Monroe could have done anything as cold-blooded and calculated as what it seemed she had. "She knew you'd said you didn't want to see my anymore. She said you'd asked her to tell me that you'd meant it."

"It wouldn't have taken a genius to guess that. She knew how terrible I felt about the accident and she must have known that I hadn't seen you much. She could have guessed at how I'd react."

"She had the necklace," he said, not so much arguing as trying to understand what had happened.

"The necklace? The one you'd given me?"

"She said you didn't want it anymore." Mitch pulled one hand out of his pocket and opened it to reveal the silver chain and heart.

"My necklace." Jenny's cry came straight from the heart as she reached to take it from him. He allowed it to slide into her palm. "I thought I'd lost it."

"I thought you didn't want it."

"How could she?" Jenny closed her fingers around the necklace and looked up at him, her eyes dark with anguish. "She's my mother. How could she do something like that?"

Mitch stared at her, groping for something to say, something to excuse her mother's behavior. But there was nothing he could say, no excuse for what she'd done.

"I don't know," he said finally.

"We've never been close," Jenny said, speaking as much to herself as to him. "But I never thought she hated me. And she must have."

"Maybe she thought she was protecting you," he offered at last, his heart twisting at the pain in her eyes.

But Jenny shook her head. "She just wanted her own way. And she used my guilt over Daddy's accident to get it. She never let me forget that the accident was my fault."

"Oh, Jenny." Mitch reached out to pull her into his arms. "It wasn't your fault. It was just a stupid, senseless accident."

"He was looking for me. If he hadn't been worried about me, he wouldn't have had the accident at all," she said stubbornly, repeating the words she'd told herself so many times, the words her mother had used all those years ago.

"You don't know that."

"Yes, I do. It was my fault."

Hearing the dogged belief in her voice, Mitch wondered what it would take to make her see how wrong she was. For the first time, he was starting to think that he might have the time to tell her.

He rested his cheek against the dark gold silk of her hair. She felt so right in his arms. It was like coming home only to find that home wasn't a place. It was Jenny.

"Oh, Mitch. All those years I spent thinking you'd just left without a word." She rubbed her face against the soft black cotton of his shirt. "What a waste."

"At least we know the truth now. That's why I came back here. To find the truth."

But more to find the woman in my arms, he thought. It was too soon to tell her that. She was still reeling from the shock of finding out what her mother had done.

"All those years," she said again, her voice suddenly thick with tears.

"Hush. It doesn't matter now." He put his fingers under her chin and lifted her face to his. "Tears won't change what happened."

"How could she do such a thing?" she whispered.

"I don't know." Mitch stroked his thumb over her cheek, brushing away the dampness of tears. Her eyes reflected the hurt of what her mother had done, a hurt that was softened by the years that had passed between then and now.

"Don't cry, Jenny." Mitch's mouth drifted across her face, tasting the salt of her tears.

Jenny turned her head until her lips met his. With a sigh, Mitch gathered her into his arms, cradling her against the broad strength of his body. They exchanged gentle kisses, kisses that helped to heal a ten-year-old pain.

Passion slid softly into their embrace, catching them both unaware as comfort became need. Mitch's head tilted, his mouth slanting over hers with new demand, his tongue stroking the soft curve of her lower lip. With a sigh, Jenny's mouth opened, her own tongue coming out to touch his, inviting him into the warm cavern of her mouth.

The kisses they'd shared after their picnic had proved that passion still ran strong and hot between them. Ten years seemed only to have fed the fires, and hunger and need formed the fuel to cause the flames to spring to life. Hunger and need formed the fuel that stoked the flames.

Mitch slid one hand into her hair, his fingers curling into the dark gold locks as his mouth opened over hers in powerful demand—a demand Jenny answered with her own.

Jenny's fingers clutched his shirt, gathering desperate little handfuls of fabric as if that were all that kept her anchored to reality. Time seemed to compress, making all the years he'd been gone hardly more than the blink of an eye. As a girl of eighteen, she'd sensed a connection between them, a bond that couldn't be denied.

As the years had passed, she'd convinced herself that that bond had been more a product of a fevered imagination than a reality. But her visceral response to his touch went much deeper than the merely physical. What was between them was something that neither time nor distance could destroy.

"Jenny." Mitch dragged his mouth from hers to look down at her, his eyes brilliant blue and full of a hunger that made Jenny feel at once terribly weak and powerfully feminine. "If this is going to stop, it's got to stop here and now."

"Who said it was going to stop?" she asked, her voice smoky with invitation.

"This isn't why I brought you here," he said.

"It's what we both want. You *do* want me, don't you?"

"Want you?" His laugh held a note of pain. "Only about as much as I want to breathe."

"Then why are we standing here talking?" Her fingers found the front of his shirt and began sliding the buttons loose.

"Jenny, wait." Mitch covered her hands with his own, stilling her fingers. "Are you sure? You're not going to hate me tomorrow, are you?"

Jenny met his searching look, her eyes dark with a mixture of regret and need. "I couldn't hate you even when I thought you'd left without telling me."

She dragged her hands free and lifted them to cup his face. "Ten years ago, my mother took something from us and now we'll never know what that something might have been."

"We can't go back, Jenny." His regret was as deep as her own.

"No. But there's still something between us, Mitch. And I think we owe it to ourselves to find out what it is."

"You are so beautiful," he whispered. Mitch's thumb traced the line of her mouth, lingering on her lower lip until Jenny opened her mouth and caught it between her teeth, drawing it inside. Her tongue swirled around the captured thumb, her gaze holding his, pure invitation in the look.

"Siren." The husky word was more endearment than curse.

Mitch pulled his thumb from her mouth, his lips coming down on hers with a hunger that said that there'd be no more questions.

It felt as if a million miles lay between them and the rest of the world. Outside, the world continued to turn, but neither of them cared about anything beyond the four walls that enclosed them.

Their clothes seemed to almost melt away as they kissed. Jenny couldn't have said just when Mitch shrugged out of his shirt, anymore than she knew when her blouse and bra disappeared. The feel of crisp chest hair teasing her nipples brought a whimper of pleasure from her. The small sound sent a ripple of response down Mitch's spine.

His fingers were impatient with the zipper on her skirt, his hands rough as he shoved the garment over her hips. Her panty hose were an intolerable barrier, and he almost growled with frustration as they resisted his impatient attempts to remove them.

"Wait." Jenny dragged her mouth from his and stepped back, despite his reluctance to allow her to put so much as an inch between them. She hooked her thumbs in the top of the hose and pulled them down her legs. Stepping out of them, she felt suddenly, self-consciously, aware that she wore only a pair of peach silk panties.

She didn't look at Mitch as she tossed the panty hose away. She wasn't eighteen anymore, she thought, wondering if he'd been expecting her to look just as she had then. Was he disappointed in what he saw?

"God, you're beautiful." The whispered words brought her eyes up, and the hungry way his gaze went over her banished any doubts she had about whether or not he liked what he saw. He reached for her, but she set one hand against his chest to hold him off.

"Aren't you overdressed for this party?"

"I guess so."

The rasp of his zipper sounded loud in the quiet room. Despite her bold request, Jenny looked away as he shoved the jeans down over his hips. But her eyes drifted back when she heard him kick the garment out of the way.

Her breath caught in her throat. He was magnificent, she thought, feeling almost dizzy. Without thinking, her hand came out, her fingers touching the hard length of his arousal. Mitch sucked in a quick breath and she lifted her eyes to his face, feeling a surge of feminine power at the look of sweet agony that twisted his features.

Still watching his face, she curved her fingers around him, feeling the silk-sheathed steel heat that made him a man. She felt his response in the way his flesh swelled still larger in her hand, as well as saw it in his face.

The one night they'd spent together, she'd allowed him to direct their lovemaking. She'd responded, but she hadn't had the knowledge or the confidence to instigate anything. Experimentally she stroked her hand over him and his breath was suddenly a harsh rasp in his throat. She'd never before realized how much enjoyment could be derived from the giving of pleasure.

But Mitch's fingers were suddenly closing around her wrist as he drew her hand away from his aching flesh.

"If you keep this up, this is going to end before it gets started," he told her huskily.

"Oh." Jenny blushed as she realized what he meant.

If Mitch had thought it was impossible to want her more, she proved him wrong. There was something wildly arousing in seeing her blush like a virgin after the wanton way she'd just been handling him.

"I think you're the one who's overdressed now," he said softly. "No. Let me." He stopped her when she reached for her panties.

He moved closer, his hands settling on her hips just above the narrow lace that edged the scrap of silk. Jenny closed her eyes, waiting to feel that last, fragile barrier disappear. But her eyes flew open again as he dropped to his knees in front of her.

His tongue found the shallow indentation of her belly button, and her hands curved over his shoulders as her knees weakened. He nibbled the soft flesh of her belly, sending wild shivers up and down her spine and setting a liquid fire in her stomach. His teeth closed over the fragile lace waistband and he began dragging the silk downward, his hands cupping her bottom as he eased the garment away.

Her legs trembling, Jenny shifted to allow the panties to drop to the floor and then cried out in shocked surprise as she felt his tongue delving between her thighs.

"Mitch!"

Her fingers clutched his hair, intending to pull him away, but the sweet delight of what he was doing made her hesitate. The hands that still held her bottom flexed, drawing her forward. The movement forced her legs to separate, opening her to him.

And she was lost.

Jenny's head fell back, her breath coming in shallow pants as he used his mouth to send wild flames of pleasure licking over her body. She clung to him, her fingers buried in his hair, her trembling legs barely supporting her.

And when her legs would no longer offer even that trembling support, Mitch eased her down, kissing his way up her body as he lowered her to the floor. By the time Jenny felt the carpet against her back, his mouth was at her breasts, finding her swollen nipples and suckling them.

Whimpering with need, she dragged his mouth up to hers at the same time she opened her legs to cradle his hips. She tasted herself on his mouth, a sweetly musky scent that made her hunger even greater.

She needed to feel him inside her, needed to feel completed in a way he alone could provide. Only then would the ache be eased, the hunger assuaged.

And then she felt him against her, burning heat and silken pressure. And she wanted.

He dragged his head up, not moving until she opened her eyelids and stared up at him.

"I want to watch you," he told her, his voice hardly more than a rasp of sound. "I want to watch your face when you take me inside."

Mesmerized by the look in his eyes, by the husky words, Jenny couldn't look away. And then she felt him entering her, a slow, steady thrust that claimed her as his and his alone.

But the possession was not his alone. Mitch felt her flesh enclose him, sheathing him in the sweetest of embraces, making him hers, now and always.

The intensity of the moment had him closing his eyes, afraid to let her see what he was feeling, half-afraid of facing it himself.

Her hands came up to clutch his shoulders as he began to move over her, slow, rocking movements that widened the liquid fire in the pit of her stomach. The flames lapped outward, consuming her with slow, burning pleasure.

Jenny's hips rose to meet each thrust, her hunger as great as his, her need as consuming. They rocked together, the rhythm growing even more wild as the flames threatened to consume them both.

"Mitch!" His name left her on a breathless cry as he felt her body tighten beneath him, around him. He withdrew and then thrust once, deep and hard, driving her into the very heart of the fire. He felt the shuddering pleasure take her, saw it in the flush that worked its way up from her breasts to the arch of her neck, before flooding her face.

He wanted to watch every second of it, savor her satisfaction without the distraction of his own. But the delicate contractions drew him deeper. With a guttural groan, he plunged headlong into the same delicious fire that consumed her.

It was a long time before he gathered the strength to roll away from her. Jenny opened her eyes as she felt him slide one arm beneath her shoulders and another beneath her hips. He rose from his knees and lifted her in one easy movement, and she looped her arms around his neck.

"This is where I'd planned to be from the beginning," Mitch said as he set her on the sheets and then slid into bed beside her. His words were half an apology for the rather rough-and-ready nature of their encounter.

"I've got no complaints," Jenny said. She snuggled her head into his shoulder, her body curving against his side. "Do you?" she asked softly.

"Have complaints?" Mitch's hand nudged her head back until he could see her face. "The only complaint I have is that it took us ten years to get back here."

"It did take us a while." She threaded her fingers through the curling hair on his chest. "I guess we have a lot of lost time to make up for."

"If that's an invitation, I'm more than willing to take you up on it," he told her, his mouth curving. His hand stroked down the silken length of her back.

"It's definitely an invitation," she told him breathlessly, arching closer to his hard body.

"Then, you can consider this my RSVP." His mouth closed over hers, smothering her small moan of approval.

Chapter 12

Jenny woke slowly. She was too warm but she didn't care. She knew immediately where she was. She was wrapped in Mitch's arms, held close against his body, which was the source of the warmth that had awakened her.

She made no effort to move to a cooler spot on the bed or to throw off the covers that were dragged over them though the hum of the air conditioner suggested that the air in the room might be pleasantly cool.

Instead, Jenny snuggled closer to the masculine furnace beside her, burying her nose in the thick mat of black hair that covered his chest. It was strange how natural it felt to wake in his bed, in his arms. This was the way it should have been ten years ago. But she wasn't going to think about that. For a little while longer, she was going to live only in the moment.

"If you keep wiggling like that, you're going to force me to take drastic action." Mitch's voice rumbled under her ear.

Keeping her face hidden against his chest, Jenny squirmed still closer, winding her arms around him. Since she could feel him hardening against her thigh, she had a pretty good idea what his "drastic action" would be. If he'd wanted to discourage her, he should have chosen a more effective threat.

"Obviously, you're a woman who likes to court danger."

"I don't see any danger," she murmured, tilting her head back to meet his eyes.

"You just don't know what to look for."

Jenny gave a startled gasp when he used the arm under her waist to scoop her off the bed and bring her against his hard frame. She shoved her hair out of her face and looked down into his smiling eyes.

She could feel him hard and heated against the soft skin of her belly. Arousal simmered just below the surface, needing only a touch, a kiss, to set it loose. Neither of them had any doubts as to how the morning would begin. But the urgency of the night before had eased, leaving them time to play, to explore the pleasures to be found in simply being together.

"I suppose you think a show of brute force will intimidate me," she said, lifting one brow in a haughty challenge. At the same time, she shifted ever so gently against him, pleased with herself when she felt his response.

"I suppose you think those beautiful brown eyes of yours are enough to keep you out of trouble."

"Aren't they?" She batted her eyelashes and shifted her legs so that her knees lay pressed against the outside of his hips.

"It depends on the trouble. They could serve to get you *into* trouble in a situation like this."

"What kind of trouble?" she asked saucily, her eyes smiling a challenge.

"Like this." Mitch's hands closed over her hips, lifting her easily. Jenny's fingers clutched his forearms as he eased her back down, sliding himself into her waiting heat.

Maybe she'd been wrong to think the urgency had eased, she thought dazedly as she took him into her body. Acting on instinct, she sat up, moaning with pleasure as the new position forced him deeper than before.

His eyes watching her, Mitch used his hands to guide her, teaching her the movement, seeing the flush of passion run up her body, tinting her skin pink. His fingers left her hips, his hands lifting to cup the soft globes of her breasts, stroking the hardening tips until he'd drawn another moan from her.

When Jenny collapsed onto his chest a few minutes later, her breath was coming in sobbing pants. A fine sheen of sweat coated both of them, their skin slick and hot with the passion so recently spent. Mitch's hand moved up and down her back, soothing the fine tremors that shook her slender body.

"I did try to warn you," he murmured in her ear.

"If that's 'trouble' I'm sorry I didn't know it sooner." Jenny drew a deep breath and released it slowly. It took every last ounce of strength in her body to raise her head until she could see his face. "You can take 'drastic action' anytime you want."

"You could live to regret that invitation." Mitch grinned at her, lifting his hand to brush a damp curl from her forehead. "Much more of that sort of thing and you're going to be too sore to move."

"I don't care."

"I do. I didn't bring you here last night to heap abuse on you." Mitch eased her off his body and set her on the sheets beside him.

"I don't feel abused." Jenny reached up to stroke her fingers over the stubble that darkened the line of his jaw as he leaned on one elbow beside her.

It was, she realized, her first experience of waking up with a man. She liked the look of him, all sleep tousled and beard shadowed. He looked like a pirate.

"I have a confession," he said abruptly, his eyes serious as he looked down at her.

"A confession?" Jenny felt a little chill in the pit of her stomach. Her hand dropped away from his face, her eyes searching his face. "What kind of confession?"

Please, God, don't let him tell me that he's married and has six kids.

"I let the air out of your tires last night," he said solemnly.

"You what?" It was so far from her fevered imaginings that it took her a moment to realize what he was talking about.

She finally remembered leaving work, only to find her tires flat. It didn't seem possible that that had been less than twelve hours ago. It seemed like a whole lifetime had passed since then.

"I let the air out of your tires and then waited for you to come out, so I could offer you a lift. And I planned to bring you back here from the beginning."

"You mean, you had no intention of taking me home," she said slowly.

"None at all." He made the admission with the air of someone clearing the slate and getting everything out in the open.

"I guess, if you're going to be honest, then I should be, too." Jenny lowered her eyes from his and nibbled on her lower lip, as if trying to find the right words. "When I came to the garage and asked you to fix that flat tire ten years ago, I'd run over a board with a nail in it. Deliberately."

She looked at him from under her lashes, attempting a penitent expression.

"I'm shocked and horrified," Mitch said, after a moment. There was a tuck in his cheek that suggested that he wasn't quite as shocked as all that.

"I know. I was a shameless hussy."

"*Was?*" He lifted a brow. "Considering your behavior this morning, I'm not sure you can use the past tense."

"I was led into temptation," she protested primly.

"*Who* led *whom?*"

"Isn't that just like a man, to blame a woman for his own weakness."

"*Weakness?*" He feigned indignation. "I didn't hear any complaints of weakness a few minutes ago."

"I was merely being polite. After all, I *am* a guest and it's the duty of a good guest to go along with whatever her host has arranged for her entertainment."

"What if her host thinks it would be entertaining to paddle her most enticing little butt?" Mitch asked, looming threateningly over her.

"Then she'd be forced to defend herself, of course." Jenny's fingers found the sensitive skin along his ribs and the conversation degenerated into a tickling contest.

It was, she thought later, an altogether perfect way to wake up.

It turned out to be just the beginning.

Though Jenny usually worked on Saturday, when Mitch asked if she had the day free, she had no trouble persuading her conscience that there was no need to go into the Works on this particular Saturday. Her parents had left the day before to spend the weekend in Denver, so there'd be no one at home to miss her. And she wanted this day with Mitch.

No matter what happened later, she wanted at least this one day to remember. She wasn't going to look at the past and she wasn't going to think about the future. She was just going to enjoy today.

Afterward she would have been hard-pressed to explain to anyone else just what it was that made the two days that followed so utterly perfect. Nothing momentous happened, at least nothing that would have seemed momentous to anyone else. But in a period of little more than thirty-six hours, Jenny learned what it was to live again.

The accident that had taken her father's ability to walk, had also taken most of her youth. Her guilt-driven need to try to minimize the effects of her father's paralysis had left her with little time for living.

It had been so long since she'd taken time off simply to enjoy herself that, had she been alone, she wouldn't have known what to do with herself. But Mitch had no such problem.

It was nearly noon when they finally crawled out of bed, propelled by hunger. But before he fed her, Mitch introduced Jenny to the pleasures of sharing a shower. The end result was inevitable and the clock's hands pointed to twelve-thirty before Jenny again crawled out of the now-damp sheets.

Laughing, she fended off Mitch's attempts to drag her back into the bed. Pleading starvation, she snatched up her clothes and fled into the bathroom, locking the door behind her. When she came out fully dressed and found Mitch waiting for her, quite magnificently naked, she felt her knees weaken.

"We could order a pizza," she suggested, her eyes skimming over his body.

"You had your chance," Mitch told her. He bent one knee, leaning slightly forward in a pose reminiscent of Greek statues she'd seen. Jenny's mouth went dry and she forgot all about her empty stomach.

"I really wouldn't mind pizza," she said wistfully. Seeing the look in her eyes, Mitch grinned and bent to pick up the clothes he'd laid ready.

"Man does not live by pizza alone," he said, walking by her on his way to the bathroom. "Besides, waiting makes everything taste sweeter."

She'd already waited ten years, Jenny thought as she watched him close the door behind him. But she'd promised herself she wasn't going to think about that. There'd be time enough to decide whether or not to confront her mother about the damage her lies had caused.

When Mitch came out of the bathroom, he'd shaved and dressed in a fresh pair of jeans and a T-shirt that just matched the blue of his eyes. Jenny felt her heart give a quick little bump.

How had she survived without him all these years? It had been like living without her heart. He'd taken that with him when he left and she'd stopped really living from that moment until he'd walked back into her life.

"Ready?" Mitch turned to look at her, slipping his watch over his wrist. His look sharpened when he saw her dazed expression. "What's wrong?"

"Nothing." Jenny shook her head and forced a smile. *Nothing, unless you count the fact that I've just realized that I'm still in love with him. That I've never stopped loving him.*

"I was just thinking about how good food sounds," she said when Mitch continued to look at her questioningly.

"If you're suggesting that I'm starving you, I'd like to point out that I was not the one who looked so delectable in the shower this morning that she delayed our meal by a good thirty minutes."

Jenny came up with an appropriate response, but five minutes later, she couldn't have said what it was. Realizing her feelings had left her so dazed that she forgot to feel self-conscious about straddling the big Harley in broad daylight. Clinging to Mitch's waist, she was oblivious to the occasional curious looks that came their way as Mitch wove his way through the streets, heading for the Monroe house.

How could she *not* have known that she loved him? From the moment Beth had told her he was back in town, he'd haunted her thoughts. And then she'd seen him and suddenly started to feel a niggling dissatisfaction with her life. She'd thought it was just that he'd reminded her of old times, but she realized now that it was so much more than that.

With her face pressed against his back, Jenny wondered how he felt about her. Was it possible that he'd loved her all these years, maybe without knowing it, the same way she hadn't known? Or was she just asking to have her heart broken again, to even think such a thing?

Her arms tightened around his waist. She'd promised herself that she wouldn't think about the future. And wondering whether or not Mitch loved her was certainly in that category. For today, it was enough that they were together, that he was hers for at least a few hours. Her lover. The future would have to take care of itself.

Later Jenny wondered at her own ability to avoid the questions and doubts that should have plagued her. It was as if, in making up her mind to take this time and think only of the moment, she'd managed to banish every other thought from her mind.

Mitch took her home to change, following her up to her bedroom while she dug through drawers, looking for the jeans she rarely wore. It seemed odd to have him in the bedroom that had been hers since childhood. Looking at his reflection in the mirror over her dressing table, Jenny found herself blushing at the sight of him stretched out on her bed, his dark jeans and blue T-shirt somehow terribly masculine against the ivory-and-sea-foam-green coloring of her bedroom.

Despite the intimacy they'd shared, she found herself edging toward the bathroom to change. Catching Mitch's curious look, she settled for retreating behind the closet door, at least while she changed into fresh underwear. Minimally covered by a pair of ivory silk panties and a matching camisole, she glanced up and caught his gaze in the mirror and realized he'd been able to see her every minute.

Cursing the fact that her fair skin tended to blush easily, she pushed the closet door shut and walked to where she'd left her jeans, her movements almost defiant. Mitch, apparently sensing her sudden uncertainty, wisely chose to say nothing.

Once outside the house, Jenny's uneasiness vanished and she found herself grinning as he sent the motorcycle roaring down the driveway. From that moment on, the day seemed made for them alone.

They had fish and chips for lunch and then wandered down Main Street, peering into shop windows and arguing in a friendly way over conflicts in their taste. It was a time for getting to know each other, the kind of day that had been denied them ten years ago.

They were just coming out of an ice-cream shop, each carrying a cone piled high when Jenny heard her name called. Feeling a twinge of resentment at the interruption, she turned, her annoyance easing when she saw Beth hurrying toward her, her two boys in tow.

"Jenny Monroe! What on earth got you out of that moldy office of yours," she exclaimed breathlessly as she stopped in front of them.

"Hi, Beth. Have you met Mitch Sullivan?"

"No. But I was certainly hoping you'd introduce me," Beth admitted. "Why else would I have dragged these two across the street at a sprint?" She turned openly curious eyes on the man beside her friend.

"Mitch, this is Beth Larkin. We've been friends since kindergarten."

"The same Beth whose mother taught you to bake burned cookies?" Mitch asked as he took Beth's hand.

"The burning was Jenny's idea," Beth said, grinning up at him. "I'm glad to finally meet you, Mitch. In fact, I'm glad to meet any man who can pry Jenny away from her work."

"Adam is trying to eat a dirt clod," Jenny informed her.

"Oh, damn." Beth grabbed for her youngest, commanding him to drop the dirt he'd pulled from a streetside planter.

"Gotta go, Beth," Jenny said, grabbing Mitch's hand. "I'll see you later."

She grinned over her shoulder as they moved away, catching Beth simultaneously frowning at her and giving her a thumbs-up.

"I thought the two of you were friends," Mitch commented as they turned off Main and walked toward a small park.

"We are. But Beth also happens to believe that honesty is the best policy, no matter who it embarrasses."

"So, you were afraid of what she might tell me about you." He sank onto the grass and pulled her down next to him.

"Terrified," she agreed cheerfully.

Mitch watched as she licked her way around her ice-cream cone, keeping just ahead of the drips. He'd never before realized how sexy a woman could look while eating an ice-cream cone. But maybe it wasn't the ice cream. Maybe it was Jenny. It occurred to him that he couldn't think of a single circumstance during which he *didn't* find her sexy.

Her tongue swirled around the scoop of chocolate ice cream and he suddenly lost all interest in dessert.

"Let's go back to the motel," he said, his voice holding a husky note that brought her gaze to his face. He saw eyes widen at what she read there. Wordless, she held out her ice-cream cone for him to dispose of.

They didn't talk on the ride back to the motel. Pressed against his back, Jenny could feel the tension humming through his body. By the time they reached his room and he was sliding the key in the lock, she felt a similar tension. The door had barely shut behind them when she was in his arms.

Seconds later, they tumbled across the bed, pulling at each other's clothing, their hunger as strong as if they hadn't touched in months instead of mere hours.

They didn't leave the room again that weekend. They made love, talked and made love again. It was as if they were trying to cram the ten years they'd been apart into two days. There was so much to find out.

Jenny wanted to know about the years Mitch traveled, how he'd made a success of his writing, where he lived when he wasn't traveling, all the things she'd never even let herself wonder about before his return.

For his part, Mitch wanted to know what had turned the spirited girl he'd known into a woman wedded to duty, how her dreams had come to be pushed aside.

"Why didn't you go to nursing school?"

They were lying in bed, Mitch's shoulders propped against the headboard, Jenny cradled under his arm. The radio that was built into the television was set to a station that played forties pop music, a mellow accompaniment to their quiet voices.

It was after midnight and most of the town was asleep. But sleep seemed an enormous waste of precious time to the room's occupants. So much time had been lost already.

"Daddy needed me," Jenny said, watching the idle movements of her fingers on his bare chest. "As I've told you, I ran errands and helped with his paperwork at first. And then, after a while, I began taking on more and more responsibility."

"Couldn't someone else have done those things?" Mitch frowned over her head, trying to understand how it had happened that her dream seemed to have become so completely lost.

"I didn't want anyone else to do them. I *owed* him at least that much. If it hadn't been for me, he wouldn't have had the accident in the first place."

"You said that before." Mitch shifted lower until they lay face-to-face. "Jenny, the accident wasn't your fault. No matter what your mother told you. It wasn't your fault."

"It wasn't what Mother said," she denied. "Don't get me wrong, she's done her best to heap on the guilt." Her mouth twisted ruefully. "But she didn't need to bother. *I* know I can't ever make up to my father for what happened."

"But it wasn't your fault," Mitch said again, wondering if anything he said could get through the layers of guilt she'd layered over herself.

"He was worried about me. He was looking for me. If I'd let him know I was all right instead of just running off because of my fight with mother, he wouldn't have been on the road that night."

Staring into her eyes, Mitch saw not a flicker of doubt. She believed what she was saying, believed it so deeply that he wasn't sure she could ever be convinced otherwise.

"Even if it had been your fault—which it wasn't—does that mean that you owe the rest of your life to your father? Is that what he'd want?"

Her eyes flickered away from his, but not before he'd seen the uncertainty she was trying to hide.

"I don't know," she said quietly. She shook her head. "Sometimes, I think..." She let the words trail off and shrugged.

Mitch didn't push for a more definite response. It was enough that she was at least considering the idea that she might not owe her father the rest of her life. Given time, he'd make her see that she could have something for herself without betraying her father.

"Why don't you just pick up a change of clothes and come back to the motel with me?" Mitch linked his hands in the small of Jenny's back.

They were standing on the front porch of the Monroe house. It was almost midnight, which was the earliest Jenny had been able to persuade him to bring her home. Not that she tried very hard to persuade him to do it earlier.

"Because if I do that, I won't get any sleep." She braced her hands on his chest, leaning back until she could look into his face. "I have an important meeting at nine o'clock tomorrow morning and my parents will be home in the afternoon."

In the glow from the porch light, Mitch's expression grew serious. "Are you going to tackle your mother about the lies she told?"

"I don't know." She shook her head, her stomach churning with nerves at the thought of a confrontation with Stephanie Monroe.

"The damage was done a long time ago, Jenny. Maybe you should just let it drop."

"Maybe. But I hate to leave her thinking that she got away with it."

"Do whatever will make you feel best." He slid the fingers of one hand into her hair, his thumb caressing the sensitive skin under her ear. "When she finds out we're seeing each other again, she's going to know she failed, or at least didn't succeed permanently."

"Are we? Seeing each other again?" Jenny's eyes were wide and vulnerable in the soft light.

She'd kept her promise not to let worry about the future intrude on the time they had together. But that time was almost over and the future seemed to be looming over her shoulder. There was a part of her that half expected Mitch to drop her off at her parents' house and then get on his bike and ride out of her life forever, just as he'd done before.

"I told you before that there's something between us, something that's lasted ten years. I'm not going away now that we've just found it again."

Jenny wanted to ask him what he thought that something might be, at least on his side. She knew that, on her side, it was love, as strong as it had been when he left. He'd said he loved her then. It was possible that what he was feeling was that same emotion. But if that was what it was, he hadn't realized it yet and she had to give him time to figure it out.

So she said nothing but only lowered her lashes, so that he wouldn't read what must be written in her eyes as he bent to kiss her.

Mitch's mouth explored hers with tender warmth, trying to tell her with a kiss, the words he knew she wasn't yet ready to hear. For ten years he'd been waiting to hold her like this, though he hadn't known it. Soon, he told himself. Soon, he'd be able to tell her he loved her. He just needed a little more time to convince her that they should spend the rest of their lives together.

For tonight, he'd let her go. But not for many more nights, he thought as he watched her slip inside and shut the door. Ten years was long enough to wait.

"You seem to be in an awfully good mood." Jake glanced at Mitch, his dark eyes curious. For the past week, Mitch's mood had been somewhat reminiscent of a starving wolverine. On Friday, he'd been taciturn and distracted. But obviously something had happened over the weekend to improve his mood. Not only was he whistling through his teeth, but the lines of tension that had bracketed his mouth had eased.

"Have a good weekend?" Jake probed when Mitch didn't seem inclined to respond to his first comment.

"Not bad." Mitch hid his grin by leaning into the engine compartment of the car he was working on. Jake's curiosity was palpable. Sooner or later, he'd tell the other man the reason for his good mood, but he was in no hurry.

"This weekend wouldn't have anything to do with Jenny Monroe, would it?"

Something in Jake's tone brought Mitch's head up. Jake was looking at him, his expression uncomfortable.

"It might," Mitch admitted slowly, a sudden uneasy knot in his stomach. "Is there a problem with that?"

"I don't know, man." Jake shrugged and glanced away. It was obvious that he was sorry he'd mentioned Jenny's name. Equally obvious that he knew the topic couldn't simply be dropped now.

"What is it, Jake?" Mitch straightened and faced his friend across the car.

"It's none of my business."

"If you've got something to say, say it."

"I told you that my wife works part-time at the Works, didn't I?"

"You said she does secretarial work two days a week. What does that have to do with me seeing Jenny?" Mitch's impatience was made sharper by the uneasy feeling that he didn't want to hear whatever Jake had to say.

"It's just that, according to everyone at the Works, Jenny's engaged, Mitch. To a guy named Ramsey. He's a vice president or something, and they've worked together for four or five years. Everybody thinks they're a perfect match, both of them devoted to the company and both of them coming from pretty wealthy families. Ramsey's from Boston, I think. Nice guy, from what Rachel's heard.''

Jake's nervous recitation trailed off. Mitch barely noticed. He was staring at his friend, reading the regret Jake felt at being the one to deliver the information.

"I don't believe it," he said finally. He set the wrench he'd been holding down on the fender with great care and reached for the rag in his back pocket. Wiping his fingers, he shook his head. "She'd have told me."

"Yeah. You're probably right." Jake's agreement was too quick and too hearty.

Was he right? Would Jenny have told him? They'd been so careful to avoid any talk of the present or the future. Neither of them had said anything about love. Yes, she'd asked him if they'd be seeing more of each other, but that was hardly a declaration of wild passion.

If she was engaged, would she have spent the weekend in his bed? If she had a fiancé, how many weekends had she spent in *his* bed? *If* she had a fiancé, he reminded himself. He didn't know that that was even the case yet. There was no sense in getting upset until he did know.

And if it were true?

He shied away from answering that question.

Chapter 13

"Genevieve, I'd like to speak with you."

Jenny had just started up to her room, but she turned at the foot of the stairs and looked at her mother. Stephanie stood in the doorway to the study, looking like a picture from a magazine article entitled "The Wealthy Relax at Home." Her pearl-gray silk pant suit was the prefect blend of the casual and elegant. A strand of matched pearls circled her throat, and not a hair of her artfully tinted hair was out of place.

Since her parents had arrived home that afternoon, Jenny had managed to avoid exchanging more than a hello with her mother. It wasn't difficult to do. Stephanie was generally no more anxious for her daughter's company than Jenny was for hers.

But now she wanted to speak to Jenny. And Jenny wasn't at all sure she was ready to speak with her. The anger she felt over discovering the lies her mother had told ten years ago was still strong.

"I was just going upstairs to change before going out, Mother," she said. Jenny brushed one hand over the simple peach dress she'd worn for dinner. Her mother insisted that the family dress for dinner. "Perhaps this could wait until another time."

"I suppose you're going to see Mitch Sullivan." Stephanie's words halted Jenny's move to continue up the stairs. She turned slowly and gave her mother a cool look.

"I don't see that it's any of your business, but as a matter of fact, I am."

"Do you really think that's wise, Genevieve?"

"Yes." Jenny left the stairs and crossed the foyer until she faced her mother. "I think it's wise. And if you want to be wise, Mother, you won't pursue this topic with me right now."

If Stephanie was surprised by the chill hostility in Jenny's words, she didn't show it. But then, she rarely allowed an expression to disturb the unwrinkled surface of her features.

"The door had barely shut behind your father and I when Mrs. Poddison called this afternoon to inform me that her daughter-in-law had seen you going into a sleazy motel with the Sullivan man. Do you really think that's wise, Genevieve, considering your position in the company?"

The cool question set a match to Jenny's temper. There was no personal concern behind it, no interest in what might be best for her. Stephanie Monroe was only concerned with one thing—herself.

"Jealous, Mother?" The sweetly sarcastic question was obviously not what Stephanie had expected. Caught by surprise, she allowed the merest flicker of a frown to cross her smooth forehead.

"What are you talking about? Why on earth would I be jealous of your tawdry affair with Mitch Sullivan?"

"Because I'm still young enough to have a life."

"Don't be absurd, Genevieve." But Jenny knew the barb had gone home. Her youth was the one thing Stephanie had never been able to forgive her for.

But rubbing her mother's face in the undeniable fact that she could never be as young as her daughter was not going to do anyone any good. Aware that they were standing in the foyer, where her father might overhear their conversation, Jenny brushed past her mother and into the study.

"Actually, maybe it's best to get this out of the way now," she said. Her full skirt swirled around her legs as she turned to face the other woman. "I thought it would be better to wait until I was a little less angry, but maybe I was wrong."

"I'm sure you know what you're babbling about, Genevieve. Unfortunately, I don't."

There'd been a time when that lift of the brow had been enough to make Jenny feel like a particularly stupid poor relation. But that was before she'd come to terms with the fact that her mother didn't love her any more than she loved anyone but herself.

"I know you lied ten years ago, Mother," she said bluntly. "I know that you lied to Mitch about me, just as you lied to me about what he said when he came here that day. Don't even bother to deny it."

"Why should I?" Stephanie seemed surprised that Jenny might have thought she would.

"You're just admitting that you lied?"

"Don't be so melodramatic. Of course I lied. I did what had to be done."

Jenny stared into the cool beauty of her mother's face, searching in vain for some trace of remorse, some indication that she knew she'd done something cruel. But there was nothing there but a faint surprise.

"Are you going to try and tell me that you did it for my own good?" Jenny asked. She wondered how it was possible that her mother's icy unconcern could still surprise her.

"No, though I don't doubt that you're better off because of it." Stephanie seated herself on a sofa that she'd had upholstered in black silk solely because the color was a dramatic contrast to her pale coloring.

"If you didn't justify it by telling yourself it was for my own good, then how did you justify it, Mother?" Jenny moved closer.

"I do not have to justify my actions. Not to you and not to anyone else. But I'll tell you my reasons."

"Thank you. It would be interesting to know why you tried to ruin my life." Most of Jenny's anger had drained away. It just took too much energy to maintain it in the face of her mother's indifference. Now she simply wanted to try to understand what had happened ten years ago to shift her life onto the path it had taken.

"Your life has hardly been ruined." Stephanie waved one slender hand to indicate their surroundings. "You've hardly been deprived of life's luxuries, let alone its necessities."

"I guess that depends on how you define necessities." Jenny sank onto a chair at right angles to her mother's seat.

She didn't try to explain that *Mitch* had been a necessity in her life, that nothing had been right without him. She'd never be able to make her understand. There was something almost pathetic about Stephanie's belief that the material things in life were all that mattered.

"Go on, Mother." She waved away the other woman's questioning look. "Tell me why you lied to me. Why you lied to Mitch."

"Obviously, you've made up your mind to cast me as the villainess in this." Stephanie lifted one shoulder in an elegant shrug. "It doesn't really matter what you think of me, but I think you should look at the facts."

"*Your* facts, you mean, the ones that explain how it was all right to tell the lies you did."

"You could whine about the lies I told, but it seems to me that being the cause of the accident that crippled your father is a transgression of considerably greater magnitude."

She slid the blade home without batting an eye, Jenny noted with some distant part of her mind. And knowing that the words were meant to wound didn't make the pain any less.

"You know just where to stick the knife in, don't you, Mother," she said, her voice weary.

"I hate to use a cliché, but the truth frequently hurts, Genevieve. And, to use another, people dwelling in glass houses should be careful about throwing stones. Like it or not, *you're* the reason your father is stuck in a wheelchair for the rest of his life. If I hadn't stopped you ten years ago, you'd have gone off with that Sullivan boy and never given your father another thought. You wouldn't have cared that the company might have collapsed."

"Is that what it was about?" Jenny stared at her, full understanding dawning at last. "You were afraid the company would go under and you'd lose a tidy little source of income. This didn't have anything to do with worrying about Daddy."

"Your father might have given up if you hadn't been here to urge him to keep going. You were so eager to be helpful, I think he kept going because he didn't want to disappoint you."

"And you didn't lose the income." Jenny stood up, unable to sit still another moment. Her stomach churned with tangled emotions. She didn't know whether to be glad or sorry that the last tiny bits of illusion had fallen from her image of her mother.

"It was your income, also, Genevieve. And your father's. In your eagerness to assign blame, don't forget your father. He depends on you now. He needs you. It was your thoughtlessness that put him in that wheelchair. Helping him keep his business together seems like the least you owe him."

Jenny closed her eyes and turned away, but there was no avoiding the fact that Stephanie's words were the cold, hard facts. No matter what her mother had done, no matter how selfish her motives, Jenny couldn't deny her own guilt.

"When I heard that the Sullivan boy was back in town, I hoped you'd have the good sense to keep your distance from him." Obviously Stephanie hadn't lost sight of her original reason for wanting to speak to Jenny.

"Since you're seeing him again, I assume that you've decided that you no longer care how much your father needs you."

"Daddy could manage without me," Jenny said wearily.

"And I suppose his ability to 'manage' makes it all right for you to simply walk away from your responsibilities toward him?"

"I'm not going anywhere." Jenny rubbed one hand over her face, trying to clear her thoughts.

"But if this man asked you to leave with him, you'd go without a backward glance, wouldn't you?" The contempt in Stephanie's voice was cutting, and Jenny felt its bite.

Her first reaction was to shout that she'd leave the minute Mitch asked. But she couldn't forget her father.

"Since he hasn't asked me, it's something of a moot point, Mother."

"Perhaps." Stephanie rose to her feet. "But you should think about what I've said, Genevieve. In this life, we can't always do what we'd like. Sometimes we have to do what's right, instead."

Jenny watched her leave the room, an ice-cold woman who'd never had anything less than what she wanted, no matter who got hurt in the process.

She sank back into her chair, her head pounding. Nothing had gone the way she'd thought it would.

There'd been no denials, no apologies for the damage her mother had done ten years ago. Instead, Stephanie had somehow turned the tables and Jenny was the one left feeling guilty.

She had to see Mitch. Just thinking about him made her feel somewhat better. It wasn't that he could make her decisions for her, but she needed to see him, to feel his arms around her. Maybe then she'd be able to think more clearly.

The summer sun lingered late and it was just disappearing behind the Rockies when Jenny knocked on the door of Mitch's motel room. When he pulled open the door, he saw her silhouetted against a background of purple-streaked clouds shot through with touches of fiery orange.

"Mitch!" Jenny stepped into his arms, her face lifted for a kiss.

He hesitated an instant, studying her features, but there was nothing there to tell him whether or not she'd lied to him. If she was engaged to some man in her father's company, he couldn't read it in the soft curves of her face. And there was certainly nothing in the yielding warmth of her mouth to suggest that there was another man in her life.

He released her and stepped back into the room, closing the door behind her. He'd just ask her, he thought. Jake's wife had probably misunderstood something. The woman who'd shared his bed for the past two days was not a woman who was engaged to another man.

He'd just ask her and then he'd be able to get rid of this churning in his gut.

"God, I just had the most hideous conversation with my mother." Jenny tossed her purse onto a chair and spun to face him, the soft fabric of her skirt swirling out with the force of the movement. Her tension was palpable and Mitch forced himself to focus on what she was saying.

"You confronted her about the lies?" he asked.

He couldn't have cared less about ten-year-old lies at the moment. What he wanted to know—needed to know—was whether or not the past two days had been a lie.

"She didn't even bother to try and deny them." Jenny paced to the curtained window and then turned and moved across the room until her path was blocked by the closet.

She continued to pace, her voice coming in staccato bursts as she told him about her conversation with her mother. Mitch stayed in front of the door, leaning his shoulders back against it, arms crossed over his chest as he watched her.

He listened, saying little. But he wasn't only listening to her words, he was listening to the meanings behind them. And what he thought he heard gave him a chill.

Jenny had sacrificed ten years of her life trying to assuage her guilt about her father's accident. She'd devoted herself to a job she didn't like, given up her own dreams, given up almost all her twenties to make up to him for the paralysis she considered herself responsible for.

Had Willard Monroe even noticed what she was giving up? Jenny loved her father, and Mitch was willing to give him the benefit of the doubt and assume that he loved her. But he remembered the girl who'd received a transfer of stocks for her eighteenth birthday. It didn't suggest that her father was particularly sensitive to her needs. Had he ever given her presence a thought and wondered why she wasn't doing the things other girls her age might have expected to do?

Or did he believe, like his wife, that Jenny owed him the rest of her life to try and compensate for his own loss of mobility?

Mitch didn't know the man well enough to do more than guess at his motives. But whether they were selfish or simply thoughtless, the end result was the same. Jenny hardly drew a breath without wondering how it would benefit her father.

If she thought it would make her father happy to marry a vice president of Monroe Furniture Works, would she hesitate to do it? The answer seemed obvious. The habit was so deeply ingrained in her that Mitch doubted if she even recognized it anymore.

And if it came to choosing between him and her father? Mitch's thoughts shied away from the answer to that question. "I can't believe she's trying to interfere between us again," Jenny was saying. She'd stopped beside the dresser and was aimlessly shifting the two wineglasses that sat there. "The minute she heard we'd been seeing each other, she's trying to ruin it."

"If your mother knows about us, it can't be too long before your fiancé finds out," Mitch said, watching her closely.

"Bill?" Jenny turned to look at him, her forehead wrinkled in a frown. "Where on earth did you hear about Bill?"

Mitch felt each word strike him as a separate blow. He'd known, on some deep, instinctive level, that what Jake had told him was true. But he'd almost managed to convince himself that it wasn't—that it couldn't possibly be true. Now, Jenny had just confirmed it for him, leaving no room for doubt.

"So you do remember his name."

Hard on the heels of the pain came a rage like he hadn't felt in years. It was the same kind of frustrated anger that had gotten him into brawls fifteen years ago. He'd learned to channel the anger over the years, learned to turn it into something productive with his writing. But hearing Jenny confirm that she was engaged to another man brought all the old anger and frustration boiling up inside him.

He was across the room in a heartbeat, his hands closing with deceptive gentleness over her upper arms.

"Just when did you plan on telling me about him, Jenny? When were you going to tell me you were engaged?"

Jenny stared up at him, her thoughts scattered by the rage that turned his eyes a fiery sapphire. If she hadn't been so absorbed in reliving the confrontation with her mother, she might have noticed there was something odd in his mood. But it wasn't until he loomed over her, his big body vibrating with tension that she realized that there was something wrong.

"There was nothing to tell," she stammered, trying to gather her thoughts into a coherent pattern.

"Nothing to tell? You didn't think it was relevant, is that it?"

"No." She'd never seen such rage burning in anyone and it seemed to choke her thinking.

"Do you sleep with him, Jenny?" His voice was silky, more frightening than if he'd shouted. "Do you make those funny little whimpering noises in the back of your throat for him the way you do for me?"

"No. Mitch, please—"

"No?" He drew her closer, his eyes blazing down into hers. "You don't whimper for him? He doesn't sound like a very good fiancé, Jenny," he said mockingly.

"He's not—" She broke off on a gasp as she felt his fingers close over her breast, burning even through the layers of dress and chemise.

"What was this last weekend? A sort of fling before you go back to him? Are you going to tell him about it, Jenny?" He caught her nipple between his thumb and finger, tugging at it softly. She felt that pull echo deep in her belly.

"Were you taking notes?" he asked. His hand left her breast but only to find the zipper at her back. Jenny murmured a protest as it slid downward, but Mitch ignored it. "Are you going to tell Bill how much you enjoyed yourself in my bed? Are you going to show him how I touched you?"

"No." She hardly knew what she was denying anymore. Her bodice had fallen to her waist, leaving only the thin silk of her chemise between her breast and his hand.

"Do you think he'll be able to make you moan, Jenny? Do you think he'll satisfy you the way I have?" Impatient with even that fragile barrier, Mitch's fingers snapped the thin straps of the chemise, baring her to the waist. "Whose name are you going to call when you climax, Jenny? His? Or mine?"

His mouth closed over hers, smothering any answer she might have given. It should have been so simple, she thought dazedly. She just had to explain that the engagement to Bill wasn't even official and that, even if it were, it was more of a merger than anything else.

But how could she explain anything when his hands were pushing her dress over her hips, leaving it to drop to the floor. His tongue stabbed into her mouth as he crowded her backward until she felt the bed against the back of her knees.

This wasn't the way it should be, she thought. But he was stealing her breath away, stealing her ability to think. She couldn't seem to put together the words to protest any more than she could find the words to explain how wrong he was about Bill.

They tumbled onto the bed. Mitch's mouth left hers but only to find the swollen peak of her breast at the same moment that his hand found the heated warmth at the juncture of her thighs. Jenny gasped, arching into his touch.

His mouth trailed across her quivering stomach until stopped by the waistband of her panty hose. Jenny heard the hose rip as he stripped them from her. There was a softer sound of torn silk as her panties were disposed of.

And then he was kneeling between her legs and his mouth found her and the rushing in her ears drowned out even the sound of her own breathless cries. He drove her upward with ruthless speed, giving her no chance to think, no chance to gather her defenses.

Jenny was sobbing as he sent her spinning out into space, her senses stripped from her, leaving only the sensation of his mouth on her to tie her to the earth.

She was still trembling in the aftermath when he slid back up her body, one hand wrenching his jeans open, freeing the swollen length of masculine flesh.

"Tell me he can do this for you, Jenny," he whispered harshly. "Tell me he can make you scream his name the way you scream mine."

He sheathed himself in her with one thrust and she did call his name as the powerful invasion sent her tumbling upward once again. She clung to him, her shaking hands seeking purchase on his sweat-damp shoulders. When had his shirt disappeared, she wondered. And then she wasn't thinking at all.

She sobbed aloud, her head digging into the mattress as she arched her neck. Wave after wave of sensation swept over her, each tossing her higher than the last until she thought she must surely drown. But the feel of Mitch's body on hers kept her anchored, even as she felt him shuddering in her arms.

It was a long time before Mitch moved. Jenny lay with her eyes closed, her mind a careful blank. As long as she didn't think about what had just happened, she didn't have to feel her heart break in a thousand pieces.

Above her, Mitch felt his rage dissipate, leaving him with a bitter aftertaste in his mouth. God, what had he done? Somewhere in the back of his mind, he'd been thinking that, if only he could prove to Jenny that what they had was unique, he could somehow avoid losing her.

Instead, he'd just driven her from him. She'd never forgive him for the way he'd treated her. He'd turned her own body against her, using what he knew of her responses to have her shuddering in his arms. Lifting himself from her lax body, he rolled to the side. He threw one arm across his eyes, filled with self-loathing.

"I'm sorry," he said at last, the words sounding hollow and empty in the quiet room.

Beside him, Jenny shivered and sat up. She slid off the bed and reached for the dress he'd stripped from her. Since he'd destroyed every one of her undergarments, she pulled the silk up over her bare body, trying not to notice how sensitized her skin felt.

Mitch rose and set about rearranging his clothes. When he bent to pick up his shirt, she saw the livid marks of her nails on the skin of his back and felt her cheeks flame.

"I've never slept with Bill," she said, speaking to his back. "I haven't slept with anyone but you. Not ever."

Mitch felt her words flick across his skin like a cat-o'-nine-tails. He'd known it. Deep inside, he'd known it from the beginning. Her responses hadn't been those of an experienced woman. He'd known it, but he'd let his anger blind him to the knowledge.

"Jenny, I—" He turned to look at her and broke off what he'd intended to say when he saw her involuntarily flinch away from him.

"God, Jenny." He stared down at his hand, feeling an unfamiliar stinging sensation against the backs of his eyes. "I didn't mean to hurt you."

"Bill and I aren't really engaged," she said, seemingly oblivious to his words. "It's something we've talked about, but there was nothing really agreed upon. It would be more of a merger than anything else. I'd have told you if it had seemed important."

"I know." He knew, now that it was too late. When Jake had told him about the engagement, all the old insecurities had come rushing back. It was something about returning to this town where he'd always been on the wrong side of the tracks. The success he'd attained in the world couldn't quite obliterate those old scars, those old feelings that he'd never rise above his reputation as a hell-raiser.

"Jenny, I'm sorry. I won't come near you again. I swear it. I'll leave and this time I won't come back."

Jenny closed her eyes, feeling his words blow away her remaining wispy hopes that they had a future. The way he'd made love to her had shocked her. It had even frightened her a little, but he hadn't hurt her and she'd never really believed he would. Even in anger, he wasn't capable of hurting her.

Now he was leaving, just as she'd been afraid he would. He was leaving and she'd be alone again.

"Goodbye." She had to force the word out past the choking lump in her throat. Clutching her shoes to her chest, Jenny snatched her purse from the chair where she'd thrown it earlier and fled the room.

Mitch closed his eyes as the door shut behind her. He was standing squarely in the middle of the wreckage of his dreams. Dreams he'd destroyed with his own hands.

Chapter 14

Jenny didn't sleep that night. She lay in bed, staring at the ceiling. Mitch was leaving and that was the end of it. And hadn't she known from the beginning that he'd go? Wasn't that why she'd been afraid to let herself get involved again?

Rolling over, she buried her face in her pillow, trying to force her mind to go blank. But there was no escaping from the endless round of questions that spun through her thoughts.

Mitch had been so angry over the idea that she had a fiancé. Surely he wouldn't have been so angry if he didn't care. But if he cared, he wouldn't be leaving. The fruitless argument continued until after dawn.

When the room started to lighten with the first gray light of day, Jenny gave up trying to sleep and got out of bed. Staring at her haggard reflection in the mirror, she wished she could cry. Maybe tears would help to dissolve the aching lump of loss that seemed to fill her stomach.

But tears remained out of reach. She showered and got dressed for the day in one of her dully conservative suits. Her sassy new haircut was scraped back from her face and forced into a bun with the aid of a fistful of pins to control the soft layers.

Jenny was grateful to find her father alone in the dining room. She wasn't at all sure how she'd react to seeing her mother after their conversation of the night before.

"Good morning, Daddy." She moved around the table and bent to kiss his forehead, her heart twisting, as it always did, at the sight of him in a wheelchair.

"Good morning, sweetheart. Mrs. Billings made blueberry muffins this morning."

"I'm not really hungry." The thought of food made her stomach do a slow roll. "I'll just have coffee."

She poured herself a cup from the silver pot on the sideboard and then moved to sit at the table.

"How are things at the Works?" he asked, setting aside the paper he'd been reading. "You're so efficient, I sometimes lose track of what's going on."

"Everything's just fine." It took an effort for her to focus her thoughts on the business, though it had virtually been the focus of her life for the past ten years. "We got a shipment of oak from Morgan and Sons. Harlan thinks it may be a little too green."

She rattled on, her voice more or less on automatic pilot as she reported what was going on at work. Her thoughts were elsewhere. Had Mitch already left? Where would he go this time? She knew he had an apartment in San Francisco, but he said he spent very little time there.

"What's wrong?" Her father's question snapped her back to the present. She blinked and looked at him, trying to remember what she'd been saying that would cause him to ask that question.

"Nothing Harlan can't handle, Daddy. He's been in touch with Ryan Morgan already and—"

"I don't mean with the shipment of oak." He waved one hand impatiently, dismissing the problem of the wood. "What's wrong with you? You're pale as a ghost."

"Am I?" She lifted her hands to pat her cheeks, her smile forced. "It's fashionable to be pale these days."

"You look like a corpse," he said with uncharacteristic bluntness. "You've been looking happier lately. It was good to see you going out a little, living a bit. You spend too much time on the business. When I heard that Mitch Sullivan was back in town and then started seeing you with a bit of sparkle in your eyes, I thought maybe the two of you were seeing each other again."

"You didn't mind?" Jenny asked incredulously.

"Why should I mind? I know he had a pretty rough reputation when he was younger, but most men grow out of that phase."

"But . . . don't you hate him?" she whispered.

"Hate him?" Willard's brows rose in surprise. "Why should I hate him?"

"Because of what happened ten years ago. Because of the accident."

"My accident? What did he have to do with that?"

Jenny stared at him, wondering how he could have forgotten. They'd never talked about that night, but she'd never doubted that he remembered it as vividly as she did.

"Don't you remember, Daddy?"

"I remember my accident very well. It was raining and the roads were slick and I took a corner too quickly and lost control. There was no one else involved. Certainly not Mitch Sullivan."

"But... but I was with him that night. If I hadn't been with him, you wouldn't have been on the road."

"I didn't know that you were... ah... with him." He cleared his throat, uncomfortable with the reminder that his daughter was no longer a little girl. "But I still don't see what that has to do with my accident."

"You were looking for me. You were worried because I hadn't come home and I didn't call." Jenny's voice trailed off, her world suddenly shifting as she saw her father start to shake his head.

"I wasn't looking for you, Jenny. I don't know where you got that idea. I worked late that night and I was on my way home. I didn't even know you weren't here."

"But you *had* to know." She couldn't absorb the idea that everything she'd believed these past ten years had been a lie. All the guilt she'd carried had been for nothing. "You were looking for me. It was my fault you were hurt."

"*Your* fault!" Surprise sharpened his voice. "Is that what you've thought all these years?" He held his hands out to her when he saw her nod. "Oh, Lord. Come here."

Jenny rose and took his hands, letting him draw her down to kneel beside his wheelchair. He brushed shaking fingers over her face.

"My accident was no one's fault, unless it was mine. Have you been carrying this guilt all this time? Why didn't you talk to me?"

"I didn't want to hurt you," she said. "I didn't want to remind you of what I'd done. I thought I could make it up to you."

"Make it up to me?" His eyes searched her face as understanding dawned. "Is that why you developed such a sudden interest in the business? Because you thought you owed it to me?"

She nodded dumbly. The impact of what he was telling her had shaken her to the core. Why hadn't it occurred to her that her mother might have lied about this, as easily as she'd lied about everything else.

All the years she'd nearly suffocated under the guilt. And it had been completely unearned. Her father hadn't even known she wasn't home that night.

"I let you get so involved because I thought it was what you wanted," he was saying now. "And you've done a fine job, Jenny. But, to tell the truth, I wouldn't mind taking it back on my shoulders. I've been getting bored and restless."

Jenny's laugh held an hysterical edge. She'd wasted a third of her life doing a job she didn't like, smothering under a load of guilt she hadn't deserved, only to find out that her father would really rather have been doing it himself, anyway.

All the pain for nothing. She'd lost Mitch—not once, but twice. For nothing.

"What is it, Jenny? What's wrong?" It wasn't until she felt her father brushing the tears from her cheeks that she realized she was crying.

"It's Mitch," she got out, feeling pain spreading through her body. "He's leaving again. And he won't be coming back this time."

"Do you love him very much?"

"More than anything in the world. But it's too late. We quarreled because he thought I was engaged to Bill Ramsey." She wiped her hands over her face, but fresh tears trailed down her cheeks.

"Well, that's simple enough to straighten out. You can tell him that you're not engaged."

"I told him, but that's not enough." She shook her head, feeling her heart break. "It's too late."

"It's never too late to try, sweetheart."

Jenny looked up into her father's eyes, seeing the love and concern there, and felt a flicker of something that might have been hope. Was it possible that she and Mitch could salvage something out of the mess they'd made?

He'd said that he wasn't leaving until he found out just what it was that had remained between them, even after ten years. Last night seemed to have changed his mind. Could she change it back?

"Go on," Willard urged. "See if you can catch him."

Jenny scrambled to her feet and then hesitated, looking down at her father.

"I love you, Daddy." She threw her arms around his neck, inhaling the familiar spicy scent, fresh tears flooding her eyes.

"I love you, too, Jenny."

Holding his words close against her heart, Jenny hurried from the house. If only she wasn't too late to catch Mitch before he left town.

Mitch glanced around the room one last time. He'd only stayed there a little while, but in some odd way, it was more a home to him than many places where he'd lived much longer. Maybe it was because this was where he'd almost managed to make it work with Jenny.

It was also where he'd managed to destroy his last chance at keeping her, he reminded himself bitterly.

Most of his things were already packed on the Harley. He lifted the notebook computer off the table and turned toward the door. His editor wanted to see the first draft of the book as soon as possible. Maybe he'd head for San Francisco and the apartment he rarely used and just lock himself in for a month. Maybe he could escape the ache in his gut by burying himself in his work.

He pulled open the door and then stepped back as Jenny nearly tumbled into the room.

"You haven't left yet," she said, sounding breathless.

"I was just on my way. Is something wrong?" She was not only breathless, she was flushed and her eyes looked almost feverish.

"No. Yes. No."

"Decisive." Despite himself, his mouth twisted in a half smile.

"I sound like an idiot." Jenny reached up to run her fingers through her hair, dislodging the last of the pins so that it tumbled around her face.

Mitch curled his fingers into his palms against the urge to reach out and touch her. He'd lost the right to do that last night. Turning, he set the computer down before he turned back to look at her, sliding his hands into his pockets to keep temptation at bay.

"Why don't you just tell me what you came to say?" He braced himself against the possibility that she'd returned to harangue him for the way he'd behaved the night before. God knows, she'd earned the right to it.

"My mother lied," she said abruptly.

"What about this time?" There was an odd sort of strain about her, a feeling he couldn't quite put his finger on.

Jenny shoved her hands into the pockets of her suit jacket and then pulled them out again, her restless movement adding to the feeling of tension she gave off.

"She lied about my father's accident. He wasn't out looking for me. He didn't even know I wasn't home."

Mitch stared at her, the realization of what this meant hitting him with the force of a tidal wave. All her guilt, her feeling that she had to sacrifice her life for her father, it had all been based on lies.

"My God."

"I don't have to feel guilty anymore, Mitch. I'm not sure I know how to behave without that." Her smile trembled around the edges and Mitch drew his hands from his pockets, reaching out to her automatically.

She came into his arms without hesitation, wrapping her own arms around his waist as she pressed her cheek against his chest.

"I can't tell you how it feels to know that it was all a big waste of time. It turns out Daddy would rather have run the damn plant himself, anyway."

Though she'd promised herself she wouldn't, she started to cry again. The feel of his arms around her and wondering if it was for the last time dissolved her control.

Mitch held her as she sobbed, wishing there was something he could say to ease her pain. What could he tell her? That it hadn't been for nothing after all? That something had been gained from it?

"I spent ten stinking years doing a job I didn't even like and I lost you and it was all for nothing," she sobbed. "And now you're going away again and I don't know where. And you aren't coming back."

Mitch felt the tight knot in his chest loosen a fraction. Maybe it wasn't too late after all.

"I'll stay if you want me to, Jenny. I was only leaving because I thought you'd never be able to forgive me after last night."

"I don't want you to go," she murmured so quietly he had to bend close to hear the words. He felt the knot dissolve, flooding him with a warmth that drove away the chill loneliness he'd lived with most of his life.

She'd stopped sobbing, but she lay against him like a tired child, her lashes in damp spikes on her cheeks. Mitch brushed his fingers through her hair, feeling love wash over him, sweet and clean.

"I love you, Jenny." If she wasn't ready to hear it, he'd just have to keep saying it until she *was* ready. "I love you."

She went very still, hardly even breathing. And then she opened her eyes and looked up at him.

"What did you say?"

"I said I love you. I've loved you for ten years. I'm willing to wait as long as it takes for you to decide how you feel, but I'm not going to stop saying it. I love you."

"Oh, Mitch." Her fingers were trembling as she reached up to trace the shadowed line of his jaw. "I love you, too. That's what I really wanted to tell you. I don't care what happened ten years ago anymore. I just don't want to lose you again."

"Lose me?" His arms tightened around her, pulling her so close that not even a shadow could have slipped between them. "You aren't ever going to lose me again."

* * * * *

Take 4 bestselling love stories FREE

Plus get a FREE surprise gift!

AMERICAN HERO

Every month in Silhouette Intimate Moments, one fabulous, irresistible man is featured as an American Hero. You won't want to miss a single one. Look for them wherever you buy books, or follow the instructions below and have these fantastic men mailed straight to your door!

In September:
MACKENZIE'S MISSION by Linda Howard, IM #445

In October:
BLACK TREE MOON by Kathleen Eagle, IM #451

In November:
A WALK ON THE WILD SIDE by Kathleen Korbel, IM #457

In December:
CHEROKEE THUNDER by Rachel Lee, IM #463

AMERICAN HEROES—men you'll adore, from authors you won't want to miss. Only from Silhouette Intimate Moments.

Silhouette CHRISTMAS Stories 1992

Experience the beauty of Yuletide romance with Silhouette Christmas Stories 1992—a collection of heartwarming stories by favorite Silhouette authors.

JONI'S MAGIC by Mary Lynn Baxter
HEARTS OF HOPE by Sondra Stanford
THE NIGHT SANTA CLAUS RETURNED by Marie Ferrarella
BASKET OF LOVE by Jeanne Stephens

Also available this year are three popular early editions of Silhouette Christmas Stories—1986,1987 and 1988. Look for these and you'll be well on your way to a complete collection of the best in holiday romance.

Plus, as an added bonus, you can receive a FREE keepsake Christmas ornament. Just collect four proofs of purchase from any November or December 1992 Harlequin or Silhouette series novels, or from any Harlequin or Silhouette Christmas collection, and receive a beautiful dated brass Christmas candle ornament.

Mail this certificate along with four (4) proof-of-purchase coupons, plus $1.50 postage and handling (check or money order—do not send cash), payable to Silhouette Books, to: **In the U.S.:** P.O. Box 9057, Buffalo, NY 14269-9057; **In Canada:** P.O. Box 622, Fort Erie, Ontario, L2A 5X3.

ONE PROOF OF PURCHASE	Name: _____
	_____
	Address: _____
	_____
	City: _____
	State/Province: _____
SX92POP	Zip/Postal Code: _____
	093 KAG